different slopes

No writer on gay and bisexual love writes with the originality, force, and beauty of Bill Lee. His "raunchy" moments (and there are many) derive from his own life-affirming sexual life, experienced in many areas that other horny men merely fantasize about. Few writers in any genre match him for quality of style, narrative structure and design, and humor. He leads his reader to exclaim: "I see that words remain more evocative than pictures!" You come away from Lee's writing as lover and life-affirmer yourself.

– Robert Peters
Author of an extensive list of books
of poetry, fiction, and criticism.

different slopes

A bisexual man's novel

BILL LEE

 PUBLISHERS   San Francisco

Published in the United States by
GLB Publishers
P.O. Box 78212, San Francisco, CA 94107 USA

Cover by
Curium Design
Cover art by Drew Willis

Publisher's Cataloging in Publication

Lee, Bill.
    Different slopes : a bisexual man's novel / by Bill Lee.
    p. cm.
    ISBN: 1-879194-21-X

    1. Bisexual men--Fiction. I. Title.
PS3562.E4355D54 1996   813'.54
                           QBI96-40248

First printing,
10 9 8 7 6 5 4 3 2 1

ACKNOWLEDGEMENTS

In choosing to set this novel in a specific time in history, I accepted the challenge of fitting fictional events into the actual history of the period. To the degree I have succeeded (regrettably not 100% of the time), it is due to a considerable extent to friends and advisors who actually lived through the times and in the places described. In particular I wish to thank my Amsterdam friend, Thomas Cashet (a noted writer himself), and my friends in Paris and vicinity (who prefer to remain anonymous) for sharing their memories of World War II and the days following that horrible conflict.

SUGGESTED READING

(Footnote numbers refer to the Preface following)

1 Hardman, Paul D: *Homoaffectionalism: Male Bonding from Gilgamesh to the Present.* San Francisco, GLB Publishers, 1993.

2 *Newsweek*, New York, July 17, 1995.

3 Vollmer, Tim: Bisexuality Returns: Is Gay Passé? San Francisco Sentinel, August 2, 1995.

4 Berube, Allan: *Coming Out Under Fire.* New York, The Free Press, 1990.

PREFACE

To my mind there is no question that bisexuality is not a term for some subset of the human sexual condition, but is the normal, expected situation for *homo sapiens* of all colors and stripes when our natures are undisturbed. Perhaps we should return in time even further, before the appearance of *sapiens*; can anyone imagine cave-men hunter groups or their predecessors, ranging distances from the cave for game, waiting until they returned to the cave to have sex with their women?

The Gilgamesh epic, which some say is our oldest recorded history as a species, assumes bisexuality as the norm. Gilgamesh and Enkidu were inseparable but brought together by their love for women. Hardman[1] termed the relationship "homoaffectionalism," but that seems to beg the question about interactive sexuality between them.

In response to the *Newsweek*[2] headline: "Bisexuality. Not Gay. Not Straight. A New Sexual Identity Emerges," we can only assume that they are speaking politically rather than humanistically. There is nothing new about bisexuality if, as I believe, that is our basic nature. It seems that obligatory heterosexuals are ready to castigate anyone who acknowledges having same-gender sex. On the other hand, leaders of groups of gay men, lesbians, and transgendered people have looked at those acknowledging their bisexuality as threats to the "pure queer societies." Tim Vollmer[3] recently concluded that "If gays and lesbians and bisexuals ever succeed in truly liberating human sexuality, hard-won gay identity and community will disappear." That seems to be the overwhelming fear, and perhaps even Camille Paglia would agree with that.

It seems necessary for us with acknowledged bisexual natures to stick our necks out — inviting a kiss on both cheeks. Even acknowledged bisexuals do not agree on some aspects of the lifestyle, if that is what it is to be called. Some bisexuals of my acquaintance have appeared shocked at the thought of mixed-gender three-ways as a part of the "scene"! It might be held that it is the only true bisexual activity.

According to an NBC-TV Documentary (Dateline, Feb. 13, 1996), the psychologist Dr. Ruth Westheimer says she thinks there is no such thing as bisexuality, but about seven million Americans would disagree with her. It is not overly simplistic to conclude that all humans are at least potentially bisexual, that some develop preferences for one gender or the other, and some remain open to and desirous of both. How does this fit the "gay gene" theory? That's an unresolved question.

Most of the bisexual writing that is taking place, and has appeared in recent years, is by women and devoted to the woman's viewpoint. Few male voices have been heard, and those that have seemed strangely sanitized or scripted by feminists' manifestos. To encourage dialogue (as well as entertain), I have invented a male character who was introduced to both genders early in his sexual maturation and naturally accepted both with equal fervor. Set against the backdrop of devastating World War II when the military was somewhat more open to homosexuality (see Allan Berube's *Coming Out Under Fire*[4]), this is the story of Matt Bristow, a grape-grower from the Napa Valley of California, who was caught up in the general fervor of patriotism after the bombing of Pearl Harbor and spent much of his service time as an Army medic in Europe. He made his own way, as must we all, developed his own set of "family values," and remained honest to what he knew to be truth, for him at least.

T he afternoon was hot and still, the sun a mirror that threatened to burn holes in my khaki shorts. The grape vines on the slope of the hill nearby sucked up concealed moisture from the baking soil and concentrated sugar inside the skins of their fruit for the ultimate sacrifice they would make for the vintners in the big houses at the head of the valley. Labor Day weekend was usually like this, once the luncheon cook fire was quenched and last year's rejected wine was consumed. Wine that wouldn't sell, that was too tart for the snooty tasters in San Francisco, was always saved for the public festivals. There were a few clusters of elders playing the usual games and the picnic grounds were strewn with somnolent bodies, old and young, to me all neighborly and familiar – except for one.

I had noticed him when he strolled into the park well after lunch had finished. Apparently from the other side of the hill, I thought. That was almost the same as "the other side of the tracks" in many cities, I realized. They grew different grapes on the other slope because the sun and winds were different. The frost arrived at different times. He was different from the rest of us. The curly brown hair that covered his head like a poodle dog bobbed nearly to his eyes as he strode by, gaze fixed straight ahead and apparently ignoring us. My eyes followed him, just why I wasn't sure. I noticed Louisa and Sueann looking after him, too, their gaze seemingly fixed on the round buttocks shifting rhythmically in the loose chino trousers. Was it true that women liked to look at men's behinds? I wondered why. But I realized that he was different.

Sueann said something to Louisa and giggled, but Louisa shushed her, blushing. The sisters were seated a few yards away at one of the redwood picnic tables, now bare except for a ketchup bottle. Sueann, shorter and more buxom than her sister, was only fifteen but already showing signs of being a little wild, as wild as the Napa Valley would permit. More than once by her snooping she had interfered with carefully-laid plans I had made to feel up Louisa on the porch swing, but then I lost interest in such intimacies for some reason. Louisa and I were little more than friends now, almost buddies; it was less complicated that way. I was aware of her puzzled looks aimed at me from time to time. I guessed she was having as much trouble understanding men as I was having in understanding women. Sueann didn't seem to be interested in the reasons for anything; just being and doing was enough for her, it seemed.

The stranger meandered toward the end of the clearing, near the far end of the pond that the WPA had built as part of the public works for our town. A lot of people, my Dad included, didn't think much of President Roosevelt's "socialistic" ideas of giving work to people who couldn't find jobs, but unemployment really wasn't much of a problem in the valley or even in San Francisco. The "socialist" Democrats were even talking of planting evergreen trees on the tops of the hills that weren't suitable for grapes, all with government-subsidized labor. Maybe when I got married and started building a family I would be interested in such things, but right now I was more interested in learning how to care for grape vines and how to have sex with women, or maybe it was the other way around.

It would seem that, with Louisa living only a short ways down the road, she and I could have struck some deal to educate each other about those things, I thought sleepily. We were the same age, had gone to high school together, and knew each other as well as two teenagers could. I supposed we would get married one of these days as everyone expected. When we graduated last June, it seemed that we would have all the time in the world, but the summer was nearly gone, the harvest was fast approaching, and the winter was always a busy time. I could tell her breasts had gotten larger because they made her older dresses fit tighter, but Sueann already had larger breasts than her sister and she didn't mind showing the cleavage between them. Even now, huddled with Louisa at the deserted table, she was fiddling with the second button on her blouse and the top button was already undone. I shifted a little uncomfortably against the tree trunk and closed my eyes. I could feel the sweat trickling down my bare chest as the afternoon droned on. . .

The trickle tickle became more insistent. Without opening my eyes I brushed my chest absently with my hand, but encountered something. . .

"Wha—?" Sueann was smiling down at me mischievously, her freckles pale in the shadow of her piled blond hairdo. "Oh, did I wake you, Matt?" she cooed innocently, twisting my chest hair with stubby fingers.

"Come on, Sueann," I growled, irritated by her childishness and brushing her hand away. "Pick on someone else." In spite of myself, there was a fullness between my legs. Could the girls see it? Louisa seemed unperturbed, watching us from her prim station on the redwood bench. It seemed I could pick up an aroma of warm girl flesh from Sueann's bare legs crouching next to me. Girls seemed to have a particular odor — or was that my imagination?

She snapped upright, pouting, but accustomed to my rejection of her teasing attentions. She had always been the younger brat in our group in school, the one to leave behind when possible, to ignore when we thought of a new lark to pursue. With a toss of her head she strolled off by

3

herself along the pond shoreline and disappeared from my view.

"When is she ever going to grow up?" I ventured to Louisa.

"Oh, well," she smiled tolerantly, "there aren't many other kids her age, so she just seems to get into trouble all by herself. The new priest seems to be having some luck in settling her down, though. She has volunteered to work part time in the church office."

"Who? Oh, that tall Italian type over there playing horseshoes?" I had become irregular about attending the little village church after my mother died, since my father didn't usually insist. I still missed my mother, even though she had insisted on using my entire name, Matthew, which I thought sounded like I was a prophet or something.

"Pretty glamorous for this little burg, isn't he?"

Father Paul Antonetti had all the girls and even the gray-haired matrons swooning, it seemed. Tall and athletic, with midnight black, wavy hair, olive skin, broad shoulders — he just didn't seem the type to preach the gospel in a rural hamlet like ours, but I hadn't thought much about it. I had to admit to recognizing the strong sense of masculinity that he exuded, however. He even charmed the old fogies with his hearty back-slapping manner.

"My parents are thinking of sending me to Berkeley," Louisa mentioned casually.

"Oh, yeah? I didn't know you were interested in college."

"Well, there doesn't seem much else to do around here. Maybe I will take up commercial art or something. It's not like I was getting married or something. . ."

The old not-so-subtle reminder, I thought. She might as well say what we were both thinking, that her parents had always expected Louisa and me to marry when we

4

finished high school. It just didn't appeal to me anymore, but it was becoming embarrassing to avoid the issue. Was there something wrong with me, I asked myself for the hundredth time? Why didn't I have that urge to get married to Louisa and start having kids like everyone seemed to think we should? At least my Dad wasn't pushing me — yet.

Fearful that she would persist and start her gentle pressuring again, I got up and stretched. "Guess I'll take a walk and work off some of that huge meal," I murmured, not inviting her to join me. Her face fell, predictably, but she didn't say anything. I wished she could find a shade of lipstick she liked, but she preferred to go without cosmetics. I sauntered off toward the pond, pleased to be alone.

The pond was muddy as usual. A few of the kids were splashing in it, oblivious to the mud that roiled up from around their thrashing feet. A few more picnic tables dotted the shore, but they were all deserted now that the meal was over. Some of the teenagers were playing soft ball in the grassy field behind me, their shouts becoming fainter as I left the main picnic area. I never really liked soft ball for some reason.

Trees grew almost to the shore in places, and then another open space would offer another picnic table, alternating with the scrubby trees mixed with ponderous eucalyptus trees brought from Australia. Their bark peeled down in long strips to carpet the ground irregularly. Blue birds and butterflies swirled through the silence of the lazy afternoon. But as I passed another group of trees to another open space, the afternoon took on a different significance.

The picnic table ahead was occupied. I recognized the curly brown hair of the stranger I had seen earlier. He was stretched out on the table, his hands under his head, a smile on his face, but he wasn't alone. Sueann stood next to the table, fascinated by the object in her hand. For some reason I slid behind a tree before they realized I was there and watched from my concealment.

At first I was not entirely sure what Sueann was doing because I could not see her hands. Then she moved aside a little and I could get a clear view. Protruding through his fly, his flesh was thick and rigid, standing almost exactly vertical, and both Sueann's hands, one above the other, did not completely conceal it. As she moved her hands up and down, the redder tip came into view, tense, blossoming, moist. It must have been an excruciating sensation, but still the young man, motionless and passive, made no move to either interfere or resist. His eyes remained closed, hands cradling his head as if ready for a nap, but gradually his lips began to lose their relaxed smile, beginning to tense and retract in a grimace he could not conceal. I noticed his feet in their very scuffed sneakers point tensely like a ballet dancer. His hips began to pump rhythmically. I think I heard a soft groan.

Sueann stopped her movements, staring at the organ in her hands, enraptured. Then she stepped up on the bench and onto the picnic table, straddling the man with his rigidity bobbing stiffly below. She gradually lowered herself, her skirts hiked up around her hips, and I could see his virility probing into the blond thatch between her legs. She guided it carefully with one hand, moving slowly in a small circle, easing the entire thickness into her body. Still the man made no move to assist, but he began to tremble under the pressure. As she engulfed him, a beatific smile developed on her face, an angelic essence that I had never seen.

Within moments he was entirely consumed, buried in her heat, and for the first time he began to move, twisting and squirming against her. Her smile became almost triumphant as she moved her hips in circular movements, never withdrawing, always pressing. The man's arms moved down at his side, and for the first time his eyes opened, gazing in apparent rapture at their torrid union. He propped himself on his elbows, still thrusting and twisting, and his groans grew louder, almost animal in their intensity.

It had now become a struggle to the finish. Sueann began to move up and down and he followed erratically. I could see his white flesh in flashes as they moved, and occasionally a glimpse of pink inner flesh of her vagina. She threw her head back, glorying in the contact, reveling in her capture. My envy knew no bounds. I gripped my own tumescence in my hand, unable to move away from the sight, my pulse racing. I did not dare to move my hand in fear that I would climax, but it would happen soon, I felt, whether or not I willed it.

"Uh – uh – yeah, oh – Christ – " the man growled, no longer the willing subject but taking charge with measured thrusts and twists that took Sueann with them. She had brought him to the pinnacle, and now it was his turn to complete the process.

"Yes – yes – yes!" her voice rose feverishly, concluding in a gurgling squeal, her legs trembling, her movements awkward.

"Yes – cum – cum!" the man almost shouted, and a moment later thrust strongly upward in a protracted lunge that buried his flesh deeply inside. Together they strained and twisted, lost together in some nirvana I had never experienced. My imagination was filling in the gaps. They were still groaning and moaning when I turned and dashed into the eucalyptus grove behind me, overflowing with lust mixed with a profound confusion. Even as I spattered the fallen eucalyptus bark with my seed with my flailing hand, I felt the instinctive guilt of the ambivalence I had experienced.

While I would have gladly changed places with the

handsome man from the other side of the hill, it was Sueann's role that I had really coveted. I didn't understand it, but there it was.

I returned to the picnic area through the woods, not wanting to meet anyone I knew, and of course I knew almost everybody. I was still shaking, at least inwardly, when I reached the tree that I had leaned against an eon ago. Louisa had joined some of the older women who were sewing or knitting or doing something domestic at another table, so at least I didn't have to face her questioning eyes. I slumped down against the tree again and tried to collect my thoughts.

I didn't know girls did those things, like coming up to a guy and taking out his thing, playing with it, and climbing on, without the guy doing anything! I had always thought that girls didn't really like sex and guys had to talk them into it if they were ever to get any, and certainly my experience with Louisa and a few other girls had seemed to confirm that. But that didn't seem to be the case with Sueann! Obviously the stranger had been very passive right up until the final moments. And then of course there was my own abnormal reaction to the whole thing, something I would have to struggle with.

Guys didn't have sex with guys, everybody knew that. I didn't really know why this was so important, but anything suggesting being queer was just asking for ridicule. Oh, sure, there was some joking around in the showers in high school, and it was apparent that guys sometimes got erections just from being around other guys in the nude, but that was OK. Anything to do with sex was just naturally stimulating. I remembered jacking off with another guy, Bruce Volberding, one day in the showers, but neither of us ever mentioned it later. It was just – two guys with erections, doing what comes naturally. No touching, of course, just looking.

8

While I was cogitating, I noticed Sueann strolling back to the picnic area. She didn't look at me this time, only passed by and strolled over to watch the men tossing horseshoes, demure as you please. She didn't seem half as ruffled as I was, and I had only been an observer. A few minutes later, the stranger reappeared from the same direction. Since he was coming toward me this time, I was able to get a better view of him.

Again I noticed his hair first. I had a momentary image of Shirley Temple as she danced around the Good Ship Lollypop with her little curls bouncing, but there was nothing coiffed or feminine or juvenile about this guy. There were faint streaks of blond mixed in the brown curls that revealed his many hours spent in the sun. His face was rather square because of broad cheek bones, but most arresting were his eyes − green with brown flecks, and they seemed to be silently laughing, either at himself or others, it wasn't clear. We were about the same age, I figured, or maybe he was a couple years older.

I don't ever remember really looking at a guy's chest before, but I couldn't help but notice the perfect symmetry and the definition of his broad chest. His shirt was open, tails flapping as he moved, and there was a gleam of sweat making highlights of his pectorals crowned with fans of brown hair. His eyes quickly met mine so I had to turn away, but not before I noticed a little damp spot in the crotch of his pants.

Perhaps he caught me looking there. Anyway, when I looked at him again he was looking at my crotch and didn't even try to hide it. I didn't think I had left any signs on my shorts, but I didn't dare look. I had really exploded back there in the woods after −

"Hi," he smiled directly into my eyes, coming to stand over me as I sprawled against the tree.

"Hi," I answered hoarsely, and cleared my throat.

9

"Pretty hot, eh?" It was just an offhand remark, but his bright green eyes still held mine, perhaps communicating something other than a comment on the weather. For the first time I noticed a dimple in his chin, just a little one. And I noticed his lips –

"Maybe I ought to get my hair cut like yours," he said unexpectedly, running his hands through the tight curls. Automatically I raised one hand to my crew cut, feeling the brush effect, and I think I blushed. My first thought was, it would be a waste of beautiful curls to cut them off, but it was the intimacy of the remark on first meeting that was distracting.

"Maybe it wouldn't stand up straight after being naturally curled like that," I stammered. Again my eyes dropped unbidden to his crotch, the memory of his huge appendage standing straight up vivid in my mind. I had a sudden urge to say, "I've seen it, you know, all nine stiff inches of it," but of course I didn't. When I looked back his eyes were still fixed on mine and his smile had broadened, seeming to include the entire world.

"Well, see you later," he waved casually and walked on. He had barely passed from view when my own "appendage" gave a mighty lurch, and I had to sit up to conceal the area. What the hell was happening here?

I could see that Louisa, bored with the sewing circle and the childish games, was returning, and I would have to make small talk. I wasn't ready for that, not now. I got up awkwardly, trying to control my rebellious cock, and started for the parking lot as an excuse to avoid conversation until I could cool down.

Our (my Dad's and mine) almost–new 1939 Mercury V-8 was still parked where we had left it, baking in the afternoon sun. It had the tear-drop, streamlined shape that supposedly provided the least wind resistance, or at least

10

that is what the advertisements claimed. It was my pride and joy. Henry Ford's comment that "Buyers can have any color they want as long as it's black" applied, of course, but the yellow-gray dust of the Napa Valley sure showed up strongly on the smooth surface. I needed something to do while I thought about things, so I retrieved a clean cloth from the trunk and started to wipe off the accumulated dust.

I had finished one side of the hood and was bending down, wiping the hub cap clean when, looking back through my legs, I saw a pair of hairy, bare legs and feet in scuffed sneakers. I straightened and turned around, startled that the subject of my thoughts was only a few feet away.

"Very nice," he said, eyes twinkling. I assumed that he was talking about the car, but then realized that he might have been referring to my ass that had been turned up pretty obviously as I cleaned the wheels. Again I blushed, tongue-tied again in this strange territory. I took the safest choice in answering.

"Yeah, it does OK, handles well. I haven't really opened it up yet."

He actually chuckled, and I realized that I hadn't made the situation much better. Hell, I couldn't do anything right around this guy. He had taken off his pants and slung them over his shoulder, now wearing only swim trunks. He had the muscular legs of a football player, I realized, and of course the straining crotch of the swim suit – well, I knew what it contained.

"I've got a bike, an Indian," he mentioned, sobering, "but I came over the hill today, down the path through the woods. I swim in the pond sometimes in the evening after work."

"Uh huh," I returned to my task, sweeping the dust from the top of the car, partially because he couldn't see my face that way. "You from Colesville?" I finally was able to ask.

11

"Near there. The family lives on the highway, but I built a cabin for myself in the woods, up there." He waved generally toward the top of the hill.

"Oh."

"My name's Craig. Craig Norman."

I turned toward him, relieved to be on safer ground now. "I'm Matt Bristow. Glad to meet you." I shook his proffered hand, a strong, hard fist. Again our eyes met, and there was a contact that I had never felt before, that I didn't understand.

"Well − " he seemed uncertain for the first time as if perhaps he had sensed something, too. "Maybe we'll bump into each other again one of these days − at the pond or − somewhere."

"Yeah," I agreed vaguely. I watched him walk toward the path over the hill. I didn't want him to leave, but I wasn't comfortable in his presence, either. I returned to wiping down the car, my mind in a whirl.

One thing I knew; I had never come down to the pond to swim in the evening before, but I was going to start tomorrow.

Y ou'll be dirtier when you come out than when you went in," my Dad had said when I told him I was going to the pond to wash up the next night. He was right, of course, but it was clean mud, I told myself. They had mud baths up north in Calistoga, and they're supposed to be healthy. So I swam and splashed around, all by myself, the only one damn fool enough to swim in the muddy pond, and finally went home after darkness set in.

The next night I kept thinking about going to the pond, but told myself it was stupid. He probably wouldn't be there, anyway. And if he was, what then? I called Louisa and took her to the drive-in over by the county line. She leaned into the crook of my arm during the show and it felt good. Her hair was soft in my face, and the familiar curves were a good fit, as always. There wasn't much conversation, but we had said just about everything that needed to be said over the years, hadn't we? She gave me a cool peck on my cheek when we got back, and that was OK, about as usual. Sueann was sitting on the porch, and so it was clear that I wasn't going to get anywhere trying to make out with Louisa, as usual. Sueann waved at me as I drove out, but we didn't speak.

The next night, Thursday, I went to the pond again. There was no one else there, of course, so I could think without being disturbed. I'd been mulling over the situation and decided it was all in my imagination, the effect the guy had on me. There was nothing special about him, just a funny kind of guy from the other side of the hill, and I happened to see something that nobody should have seen, because it was nobody's business, and maybe I ought to switch my attentions to Sueann so at least I would get some sex but that wouldn't set well with Louisa or anybody else, and —

And then he appeared suddenly, towering over me as I lay on the grass, letting the muddy water dry on my skin. The sun was low, just a rim of red over the western range, and the mosquitos were starting to bite, but I forgot all that when that full-mouth grin of his lit up the night.

"Hi, Matt," he said casually, as if he expected me to be right where I was. "I missed you last night."

I couldn't tell him I had come on Tuesday, hoping to find him. "Oh, Louisa and I went to a movie," I answered without thinking.

"Oh, Louisa, eh? She's the tall brunette, right? You two a steady thing?" As he talked he was stripping off his clothes, and he didn't stop with his shorts. Everything came off with no apparent embarrassment at all. I looked away so I wouldn't stare at him and perhaps betray what I was really most interested in.

"Uh, well, I guess we expect to get married one of these days," I choked, staring fixedly at a point to his left.

"Oh, got it all figured out, eh? That's great!" He sounded happy for me. Maybe it was OK after all. Suddenly I wanted him to object, to talk me out of it, to — what did I want him to do? Ignoring my plight, he turned and padded down to the water, leaving me to stare after him, watching his trim butt roll with his steps, and noting how much broader his shoulders were than his hips. Not really Tarzan, but something close. Then I became aware of something else; although his skin was fair, he had a good tan but no tan line and his butt was the same shade as his shoulders.

He shouted and waved at me to join him in the pond, but I shook my head. I didn't know what might happen if

I got close to — whatever was upsetting me about him. He didn't stay in long, and soon came striding back, dripping. He shook his head like a dog and the brown curls just bounced right back in place, as I somehow knew they would. I didn't like a lot of hair, which is why I had mine cut crew style, to avoid fussing. I tried to avoid looking at his crotch, but I still registered that he was circumcised, as usual, and it was hanging real low. I was relieved when he put his pants on, although still dripping wet; they clung to his muscular legs, and his cock pouched out obviously, but at least I could look at him without blushing. He dropped to the grass beside me, stretching out on his back.

"You live with your family?" he asked.

"Yeah, outside of Napa. My Dad has a pretty big vineyard, and I work alongside. My Mom died last year."

He grunted "Uh," in a kind of sympathetic tone, and let it rest. I liked that. We were silent for a while, listening to the crickets and the breeze in the tree tops. The sun was gone and the fireflies darted hither and yon. It was still warm but the night chill was creeping in.

"You two get along OK?" he asked somewhat mysteriously, I thought.

"My Dad and I? Sure, I guess so. We don't talk much, and sometimes argue about the best way to do things, but nothing special. I guess he's lonely since my mother died. I think he has a girlfriend in Sausalito, or maybe it's Mill Valley, I'm not sure. He usually goes to visit her Saturday nights."

"What do you do on Saturday nights?"

It was kind of an odd question, but the answer was easy. "Oh, sometimes Louisa and I go to the movies or listen to the Hit Parade or something, nothing special. Dad's usually got the car."

"You doing anything this Saturday?"

15

"Nothing planned, why?"

"Well, I'm invited to a party with some friends in Guerneville, and I just wondered if you'd like to come along. I could pick you up on the bike."

My heart jumped a little. He really wanted to see me, get to know me, other than just − casual, like this. I felt warm all over, even with the cool breeze making goose pimples on my bare legs. But what would Louisa think if I didn't phone her?

"Sure, I guess so," I answered anyhow. She and I weren't married yet, after all.

We lapsed into silence. He was so damn friendly and nice, and I was starting to feel guilty about my secret. It was eating at me. Before I could stop myself, I blurted it out: "I saw you, the day of the picnic."

"Huh?" he asked as if coming back from another world.

"On the table over there − with Sueann."

Craig quickly turned to me, propped up on his elbow. "Oh, yeah? She's pretty hot, but I didn't think anyone else was around. It was her idea." His eyes gleamed green in the twilight, searching my face to see how I felt about it. "She's not your girl too, is she?"

"No, no," I assured him. His attitude seemed pretty strange, I thought. As if sharing the experience with me was enjoyable somehow.

"Sometimes it really works out to have the girl on top, you know? Sueann seems to have been around. Have you ever − ?"

"No, no, never, I mean I never − " I sat up quickly, flustered. I was glad he couldn't see my face clearly. "Well, guess I'll be going home," I began.

"Oh, sure, Matt," he sounded a little disappointed, but also stood up. We started for the parking lot where I'd left

16

the Mercury. "If Saturday's OK, I'll pick you up about 8:30, OK? That is, if you tell me where you live — " Why did my brain always get rattled around him? I quickly explained how to find our house, and got into the car. Before driving home I watched him take the path through the woods that led up the hill. He turned once and waved before disappearing into the darkness. I drove home in a daze.

As expected, my Dad left in the Merc about 7:30 Saturday night, and about 8:30 a lone headlight groped its way into our driveway. I met Craig at the motorcycle. This time we were both dressed in Levis, boots, and leather jackets, and Craig had a helmet for me to wear if I wanted to. I noticed that he wasn't wearing one, so also demurred. Of course we all lived and worked in Levis, but I never saw anybody look so sexy in them before, and the leather jacket seemed to add something — I didn't know what it was.

The motorcycle was stripped down but still heavy, and the buddy rider seat was hard as a rock. It wasn't the first time I had been on a bike, having owned one for a while as a young teenager, so I knew how to lean on corners and such, but I was a little skittish about riding close to him all that way to Guerneville. What if I got an erection again?

Craig told me to wrap my arms around him as we set off. He had a really narrow waist, and his belly was hard as a board. I was very aware that my fingers were only a couple inches away from his crotch and all that involved. I was pretty tense for the first mile or so, but he was obviously an experienced driver, although faster than was perhaps wise. By the time we started west on the Russian River road I was actually snuggled to him, my chin on his shoulder and his chest in my embrace. I felt like we could go on this way until dawn if we wanted to.

It didn't take that long to reach Guerneville, and then we turned off on a dirt road, finally turning in at a log house set back in a grove of redwoods along the shore of the river. There were already several cars and motorcycles there, and we could hear music through the open doors. I was almost reluctant to release him from my arms, but he didn't seem to notice. Craig's face was unusually bright, both from the windy ride and the anticipation of the party, I suppose. We walked to the front door and entered without knocking.

"Hey, Craig, baby!" was the first response I heard as we entered. A huge furry bear of a man dressed in skimpy shorts engulfed him in hairy arms and kissed him heartily on the lips! This was especially startling because he had the damaged face of a prize fighter and what appeared to be a two-day beard. There were perhaps a dozen people there, all young men, and most of them were apparently old friends of Craig's as indicated by their effusive greetings. Craig tried to introduce me but in the confusion and the noise of music and laughter, I didn't really catch the names. What did catch my eye immediately, however, were two men dancing together on the back porch overlooking the shimmering river.

When Craig had gone the rounds and cold beers had been pressed into our hands, we were finally able to talk but I didn't know what to say. I had never been to a party like this before, but Craig seemed right at home. He kept his arm loosely draped around my shoulder, and I was grateful for that; after a while I also realized that that gesture had some proprietary significance as well. That made me feel warm and uneasy, both at the same time.

The chatter was extremely varied from one small group to the next. As we wandered through the party, the conversations overheard ranged broadly from Hitler's invasion of neighboring countries in Europe, Sinatra's success in concerts and records, the Germans' bombing of London, and whether bleaching Levis was too obvious a signal of one's sexual proclivities. The party spilled over into the back yard, bordered by the river. The music carried sweetly through the still air — "From the Bottom of My Heart" with Harry James.

"I like Harry James, but that skinny crooner, Sinatra, will be a flash in the pan," Craig commented.

The host, Roger, had long blond hair and tattoos all over his arms. After we'd been introduced and started to move on, Roger casually patted Craig's ass in a pretty friendly way. Craig shot him a smile over his shoulder but continued walking with me. Craig said Roger owned a large real estate business in the City, and he thought that the Russian River region was a perfect place to develop for vacation homes. It didn't sound very likely to me. A few minutes later he and Craig went into a huddle a few feet away, and then Roger passed out to the guests some thin, rolled joints of marijuana that Craig had passed to him. "I grow it outside my cabin," he explained to me. "They are just coming to harvest now, so these buds should be really good." He lit one and led me to the edge of the river to look at the view.

"Do you smoke?" he asked somewhat hesitantly, passing the joint to me.

"It's not the first time," I answered, sounding more confident than I actually felt. The plants grew like weeds between fields and vineyards and on the edges of the woods, but I guess some people were trying to improve the quality by experimenting. Practically everybody in the valley smoked pot at some time or other, but I was never impressed. In high school after football games or such a bunch of us would get high and do crazy, silly things, but then the fun wore off and we became sleepy and I hadn't tried any for some time. I found that it made me relaxed and yet excited somehow, and the combination wasn't always good. At this point I was already pretty excited and confused, being with Craig who seemed to constantly keep me off balance, and my shock at seeing guys dancing together – what the hell, smoking pot on top of everything else, why not? I took a drag and drew it deeply into my lungs, but I wasn't prepared for the wave of pleasure that encompassed me almost immediately.

Craig took another drag and, trying to hold in the smoke and talk at the same time, grunted "Pretty good, eh?" I took another toke and sat down on a log on the bank of the river, my head clear but suddenly without a worry in the world. "Yeah," I breathed, lapsing into silence again, a big smile on my face.

"You OK?" Craig asked, sliding down beside me, the remainder of the joint smoking in his hand. I think we sat together, looking out over the gently rippling river snaking its way toward the Pacific, for several minutes or maybe longer – you lose track of time on pot. The music from the phonograph changed from Carmen Miranda's crazy antics to become softer and more mellow, and there were now several couples slow dancing on the porch, gliding paired shadows blending at times into single manly shapes, the nearly full moon smiling down benignly. Duke Ellington was plaintively complaining, "I've Got It Bad and That Ain't Good."

But finally I looked at Craig, really looked at him this time, at the green eyes with brown flecks, the manly but sensitive face, and the lips – I had almost forgotten how full and expressive his lips were. "I don't know," I answered his question vaguely, still memorizing his features. "Do you think I am?" He turned on that broad smile of his and looked me in the eyes. "I think you're really OK, yeah, I really do."

His hand found mine and the warmth of his touch urged

me on. I suddenly felt free and unburdened, and there was nothing wrong in just being myself; I began to think and respond based on what was truth and what was uppermost in my mind, I guess, rather than preconceptions. I focused again on his lips.

"I'd like to — that is, if you think it's OK — I mean, your lips are so — may I kiss you?"

For the first time, a trace of uncertainty entered his eyes, and he stiffened slightly. "Now, wait a minute — are you sure, I mean, really sure you — " He released my hand, and I felt lost for a moment. "You don't have to — you know — do anything just because the others are — "

"I know," I broke in, moving toward him, but he moved away on the log. "I want to. I, uh, want you!" There, I'd said it, only vaguely recognizing what the statement portended.

Craig rose to his feet, staring at me. "Now wait a minute," he repeated, "You don't know what you're asking — I mean saying — " I jumped up with a cry, "Yes, I do!" but he was moving away, looking back at me uncertainly. I went after him, and we began to circle the log with me almost chasing him, insisting that I knew what I was doing and he shaking his head as if cornered. Then he made a dash for the house, and I darted after him.

As I reached the door through which he had disappeared, my way was abruptly blocked by the "bear," a sloshing beer can in his paw. I vaguely noticed that the inadequate shorts had been left behind somewhere, but his hairy belly was enough to completely block the door. "Whoa," he rumbled as we almost collided. "You chasing somebody?" I nodded. "Anybody I know?" His face wore what may have passed as a frown, but was even more intimidating because of his broken nose.

"Yes, I'm after Craig," I answered impatiently, trying to

get around him, first on one side and then the other. "I want to kiss him."

The huge shape moved back courteously with a belly-quaking chuckle, bowing and waving me on. "Sounds like an eminently reasonable idea to me. Go get him!"

By the time I got inside the kitchen, Craig had disappeared, of course. I started down the dim, carpeted hall, but with no lights to guide me I simply entered the first room I came to. It was the dining room. In the dark I was able to make out two figures, one leaning against the large oval table and one kneeling between his legs on the floor. Neither was Craig, nor did they pay any attention to me. The next room was a bedroom, and I wasn't sure how many guys were there nor exactly what they were doing, but there were several piles of clothes on the floor and a lot of heavy breathing and agitated movement on the bed. I had a brief urge to throw myself into the middle of the mélange, but that really wasn't what I wanted at that moment. Only Craig would do.

As I returned to the hall, I came face to face with him as he left the bathroom. We were both startled, but before he could escape I gripped him by the shoulders and plastered him against the wall, pressing my lips to his triumphantly. He was sweet and masculine — and trembling, almost as much as I. I could feel first his instinctive withdrawal and then gradual acceptance, followed more quickly with a warming passion that soon swept us both into a muscle-snapping embrace. Our tongues prodded and probed, tasting deeply, demanding, welcoming invasion of innermost secrets. When we broke the contact, breathless, we both slumped to the floor in the hall, and started all over again. Gradually he took the lead and stretched me out on the carpet, possessing me with his lips while his hands roamed over my body.

The "bear," with the compliant figure of a much smaller

22

boy nestled easily in his arms, stepped over us with a polite "Excuse us, guys" and entered another dark bedroom. His hairy, stubby hardon was pointing the way. The door closed behind them, but we were too involved to pay much attention. Vaughn Monroe was singing it for me: "Racing With The Moon."

We ended up somehow on the floor in a walk-in closet. I learned that night that many of my past fantasies could be realized, and even some that I had never entertained, but it was better if scattered shoes on the floor were cleared away first.

A bout 8 AM the next morning, Craig and I, on the trusty Indian, rode somewhat breathlessly into my driveway, only to find my father alighting from the Merc looking almost as bleary-eyed as we did. From the front door we were confronted by the stern countenance of our Latina housekeeper, Maria, her hands on her hips. I think my Dad felt as guilty as I did, that we had been out all night. I was pretty sure, however, that we had spent the night doing different things. Well, maybe not so different — to each his own. I had learned that from Craig.

At least it gave me a chance to introduce Craig to Dad, an important step, I thought, because Craig had suddenly become very important to me. They seemed to get along fine, but on a superficial level, of course. Apparently Dad didn't want to talk about what he had been doing with his girl friend in Sausalito or Mill Valley or wherever, and I wasn't really interested in detailing our adventures, either, so we took the obvious course and ignored the whole thing. A few times I caught my father looking at me a little strangely, but I think that was because I was suddenly so happy; actually I felt as if the world had lifted from my shoulders, although I hadn't been aware previously that I was unhappy. Craig called that "understanding yourself," and he was right, of course. Only Maria, a fixture to the household, seemed disgruntled that morning, grumbling and harrumphing as she served the three of us breakfast; we all seemed to be ravenously hungry. Dad looked pretty happy that morning, too. It was a rather strange threesome around the breakfast table that Sunday morning, but you couldn't tell by watching us that the reasons for our good moods were quite different in detail.

"Well," my Dad said to me over our second cups of coffee, "we had better get cleaned up and ready for church." He seemed to think we both needed church that day for some reason.

My face fell. "Oh, I thought maybe Craig and I would do something today — I mean I didn't mention it but — " I looked at him for support. We hadn't talked about the future at all; the present was all-engrossing for me.

Dad was starting to reply but Craig cut in. "Your Dad's probably right, Matt. I ought to get home myself. We can make it some other time."

I felt crestfallen, and I guess I looked it. Now that I had found Craig I wanted more, more! But he didn't seem as enthusiastic. Maybe he was bored with me. Or maybe I wasn't very good sex. I know my teeth might have scraped a little before I got used to the thickness, and once I had gagged before I could manage to take it all —

Dad was watching us with a peculiar expression on his face, I thought. Had Craig's and my behavior seemed too friendly? Too intimate? Did it show, that I was queer? I was starting to learn to be careful. The morning's glow was fading.

I followed Craig to his motorcycle in the driveway. "When will I see you?" I asked him when we were out of earshot. "How about at the pond, tomorrow night?" he suggested. I nodded. Already I felt deprived, but I didn't want to pout about it. I was no child, after all. I watched him out of sight. I hadn't even been able to kiss him goodbye since we could be seen from the house. I really liked to kiss Craig. It made me feel warm and loving and excited, all at the same time.

The church service was a major anticlimax to the previous night, and that was putting it mildly. All during the singing and the prayers and hymns and sermon, my thoughts were consumed with Craig, and also other memories of the previous night that stirred both my mind and my cock. Dad and I sat with Louisa and Sueann and their parents as usual, but I guess I wasn't much company for Louisa. I didn't pay much attention to the sermon either, of course, but afterward, as we left the church, I noticed how the congregation really fawned over the new priest, shaking his hand and complimenting him. The women especially gushed when he looked at them with those big, brown eyes and held their hands. It was disgusting, I thought. Maybe I was just jealous.

That afternoon, Dad and I, both feeling a little sheepish, I think, took an unaccustomed nap to recover from the previous night. I don't know about him, but I know I played with myself twice, practically filling a towel I kept by my bed, thinking about Craig and – everything. Maria might be a little surprised from here on by the increased number of towels in the laundry, I thought with a smile as I dropped off to sleep. I really had something to fantasize about now.

The next day a couple of people from the vintners came and sampled the grapes, both by tasting and with their chemicals, I guess. I never understood exactly what they looked for, and it wasn't clear that they really knew, either. Selecting grapes for wine was still pretty much an art. Usually I was intrigued by their sampling, but that time I couldn't get very interested. My thoughts were set on the night to come and my next meeting with Craig.

"Where are you off to?" Dad asked as I started to drive away that night. He didn't usually ask many questions when I took the car unless he needed it for something.

"Oh, to swim in the pond. Craig said he might be there," I said as casually as I could. He looked a little askance at me.

"What's this sudden friendship with Craig? He seems

a nice guy, but you seem sort of − I don't know − excited around him."

I know I blushed. I guess I had to pretend more, I thought. I wasn't used to lying and it didn't come easy. I started to get angry.

"Nothing special," I grunted, looking at the ground. "You need the car tonight?"

"No, I guess not − " I knew he wasn't satisfied but I drove off, heaving a sigh of relief. I forgot all that when I found Craig waiting at the deserted pond, in the little clearing we were beginning to call "ours." I fell on him, pinning him to the ground and attaching myself to his lips, feeling complete again. It wasn't long before we were naked and gobbling each other, starved for that contact that had become my ultimate delight. By the time we were ready to rest, at least temporarily, night had fallen and a cool breeze had sprung up. That was our excuse for holding each other, our legs and arms intertwined.

"I should warn you," Craig murmured, "I have a thing for blonds."

"Oh, yeah?"

"Hummm. Blond guys have the nicest, juiciest nipples − " his tongue and teeth focused for a moment on one of mine "− and the best tan lines." He gripped both my buttocks possessively, and awoke a bunch of fantasies as yet unfulfilled.

"Yeah?" I pretended to fight him off. "Speaking of that, I noticed you don't have a tan line. Do you go around nude up there on the hill?"

"Most of the time. There aren't many visitors," he answered dryly, resting his head on my chest.

"What is your house like?"

"Oh, it's just a log cabin, really, on the far end of our property on top of the hill. One room, with a fireplace and a well and a shower I rigged up. There's a bike trail leading up to it. I'll take you there one day."

There seemed to be so much I wanted to know about him, but I realized that maybe I shouldn't press too hard. But I had to ask: "What led you to build a cabin way up there?"

Craig hesitated and then sighed. "Well, My Dad and I don't get along all that well. I graduated from high school two years ago, and I guess he thought I was kinda wild. He, uh, decided he didn't like the way I was living my life, or something – " Craig seemed to be groping for words " – and so it seemed better that way. I still work with his crew in the vineyard, just like any other laborer, but we don't talk any more than necessary."

"That's tough," I said quietly.

He propped himself up and looked closely at me. "You may not realize it yet, but if other people find out you have sex with guys, you're in trouble, believe me. And that probably includes your father." He was deadly serious, almost bitter. Was this the underlying cause for the problems with his father?

I sighed. "Yeah, I think he's already getting a little suspicious. I've got to pretend that we are just ordinary buddies, but I hate to lie. Why does it have to be that way?"

"I don't know, it's weird. What difference should it make to them, anyhow? It's not like we are hurting anybody or getting somebody pregnant or something."

I couldn't remain so serious for very long, not with him in my arms. I quieted his mouth with my lips and that led to a lot more. It was close to midnight when I returned home.

Over the next few weeks we met whenever we could, and it seemed to me that my life was just a blur except when we were together. Although harvest time, always a busy, backbreaking ordeal from dawn to dusk, descended on us, we still found time to snatch an hour together some evenings, once on the deserted beach at Stinson, wrapped in blankets, and sometimes in the car when it was too cold outside under increasingly cloudy skies. There was an early frost that year that worried us for a while, but there wasn't too much damage and it should be a reasonable year for the wine, it was thought. Craig and I both worked our respective vineyards, along with the migrant workers and our own crews. A few times we both fell asleep in the car after sex, weary and bleary-eyed, comfortable in each other's arms.

Poor Louisa was confused by my inattention. I felt guilty when I ignored her, but I felt no spontaneous wish to see her, either. Dad started talking for the first time about when I was going to settle down and get married, although previously he had cautioned about getting married too young. However, there was the draft, I reminded him. With the war heating up in Europe and the Japanese diplomats making trouble in Washington, all young men had registered and we were all classified by local draft boards for induction into the army. No one knew how this was going to play out, nor did we feel confident in making plans for very far ahead.

By mid-November the major work was finished and Craig and I had more time to be together. We were both becoming uneasy about the need for hiding our relationship (we never really talked about "love"), and my impression that Craig was being secretive began to cause irritations when we were together. Then one Sunday, an unusually warm, sunlit day, he picked me up on the bike and we rode to his parents' vineyard. It seemed similar to my family home, but instead of taking me to meet his father and mother, he turned the bike into a nearly concealed dirt trail that led into the wooded hillside and up to the crest. We had had only one rain so far, so the trail was very dusty; the bike slid around, searching for a grip in the loose soil, but Craig was an expert biker and very accustomed to the vagaries encountered. Eventually we arrived at a tiny clearing where his log cabin stood sentry over the rolling green and gold hills of the Napa Valley.

The cabin was small, but there was a kitchen of sorts and a large mattress on the floor. A stone bed of coals with a metal hood and pipe extending through the roof filled one corner. There were half-burned large candles on the shaky table, his only source of light. He watched my face, obviously worried that I would find the cabin too primitive, but in truth I envied his independence and said so. When he was convinced I was not going to criticize, he kissed me thoroughly and lit a joint, part of his fall crop.

We stood side by side, looking out over the land that we felt was ours, sharing the marijuana and the profoundly peaceful spirit of the hill top. His arm was around my shoulders, and I could see he was proud of his work and happy to be with me. By this time, after over two months of relationship, we didn't tackle each other, stripping off the other's clothes and start having sex as soon as we saw each other, but it wasn't long before our need for each other led to the big mattress and total nudity.

Craig laid me out on the mattress, and crouched over me. I could see love in his eyes. He was playing with my chest hair as he began to tell me all the things he liked about me. It was embarrassing.

"Aw, come on," I interrupted, blushing. "You're the one who's beautiful," I insisted.

Craig shook his head firmly, "You just don't realize how attractive and sexy you are. Handsome face, that crisp, blond, crew cut, and a swimmer's body, All American Boy! And of course this huge – " gripping my towering sex.

I still didn't believe him, but I liked to hear him say it. I drew him close and gave him a protracted kiss.

The sun streamed a yellow path through the open door; when we looked out we could see white, puffy clouds drifting by and catch glimpses of hawks circling in their quest for field mice. Blue jays were raucous in their arguments in the trees outside, but there was only contentment mixed with joyful anticipation in the cabin. Craig's muscular body was warm in my arms, and when I moved lower, he was thick and sweet in my mouth; he was murmuring his satisfaction in returning my love. We were approaching our first major climax when I became aware of a shadow at the door and looked up startled. A young woman, barely more than girl, barefoot and wearing a limp cotton house dress, stood in the doorway, blinking into the dimness of the cabin.

Craig also looked up, but was apparently not really surprised. He didn't even seem particularly annoyed. The girl was quite beautiful, slim but voluptuous body, straight black hair draping over her shoulders, and a rather piquant face with full lips. She was serious and calm, almost withdrawn, as she looked without expression at us in our obvious sexual postures.

"I told you I would be busy," Craig said in a gentle, patient tone. She remained in the doorway, her eyes searching his face but showing no embarrassment. Then she turned her gaze to me, first to my face and then my erection, but made no move nor did her expression change. She returned her gaze to Craig as if awaiting instructions.

Craig sighed briefly and beckoned her to come in. She entered with a peculiar, gliding gait, almost catlike. Craig patted the edge of the mattress and she squatted at that spot, her face expressionless. "Matt, this is Daisy," he said softly. "She never speaks, but I know she understands everything, perhaps more than we do. She came to me out

31

of the night, last summer, soon after I built this cabin, and apparently has nowhere else to go. She is very loving, despite what I think must have been a horrendous past."

"Hello, Daisy," I said, smiling at her, not knowing how else to respond. Then I looked quickly at Craig. "Yes," he chuckled at the inquiry on my face, "'Daisy' after Daisy Mae in the Li'l Abner comic strip. She seems such a free soul if you don't look beyond the surface. And she prefers to go barefoot."

Craig was looking at me but speaking to Daisy. "Daisy, would you like to dance for us?" Something happened in her eyes but her expression remained passive. Slowly, gracefully she rose to her feet and began to dance slowly, sinuously, to music only in her head. Her movements reminded me of what I understood to be gypsy, although I had never actually seen a gypsy dance, of course. Her skirt billowed out in a circle when she twirled, revealing bare legs and thighs fit for a Hollywood movie star. I actually thought of Alice Faye, but Daisy had dark hair. Gradually her tempo increased, the dance becoming more and more athletic. Suddenly she swooped down and, gathering her skirts in her hands, whipped her dress off over her head, leaving her naked. Her more than ample breasts pointed upward, and her waist was tiny, swelling to perfect hips that framed her dark pubic bush.

Her dancing became even more suggestive, her hands caressing, her head thrown back at times, her legs spread and trembling, and then bowing low, her long black hair almost concealing her body as she bent forward in humility. Back and forth in the confined space by the mattress she pranced, rotating and pirouetting. Although I had been startled by her entrance and started to lose my sexual excitement, her dance reawakened the powerful drive I always felt with Craig. My body seemed to surge in time with her movements, and my erection grew almost painful in intensity. Craig was having a similar reaction and, when our excitement became too disturbing, he stood up on the mattress. His nudity was statuesque, his magnificent legs taut, shoulders braced, his hardon full. When she saw this she made one last whirl and literally leaped into his arms. He caught her gracefully, her legs around his waist, and their lips met with obvious longstanding intimacy. Slowly he eased her to the mattress next to me and stretched out beside her on the other side.

I had never been close to a naked woman before. Her skin was smoother than I was used to, perhaps because it was hairless except in select spots. She was breathing deeply, short of breath from her dance, I thought, but then I realized that she was excited, perhaps as much as I. Her eyes sought mine, a small frown between them, but when I smiled they softened trustingly. Craig watched us together, his hand soothing her brow reassuringly.

"She has fine breasts. She likes to have them stroked and kissed," he murmured. Almost in a trance I touched her breast, the firm spongy texture intriguing, and watched the nipple move in reflex. Craig's fingertips smoothed the firm flesh on his side and moved to encircle the nipple. I followed suit automatically, and when he bent to clasp it in his lips, I did the same. Our heads moved side by side, touching sometimes, as we paid homage to her breasts. Her eyes closed, obviously enjoying our gentleness. It was so different than with Craig; I frequently nibbled on his nipples, sometimes playfully causing minor pain, but Craig's nipples were crowns for his muscles, little surrogate, symbolic erections. Her's were nurturing organs doubling as erotic zones.

The remainder of the afternoon was composed of ambiguities, opposites attracted and compared. At first I was confused but gradually understood sexual complexities

33

that I had never even considered before. Craig was naturally a leader, strong, firm, outreaching and positive. Daisy was recessive, tender, soft, rounded, and inward directed. The burgeoning erection that symbolized Craig, and in essence most men, had its counterpart in Daisy's vagina, but the differences merely called for modifications of approaches to them rather than rejections of either. The actual mechanisms of relating to people sexually must differ according to the object of the sexual feeling, but I felt no guilt for either direction of expression, nor was one more satisfying than the other in general.

That was the first of several afternoons of "triple-play," as we called it from baseball jargon. On cooler days the fireplace added to our comfort, shedding warmth and flickering light to our pleasures. I also learned to derive the optimal pleasure from giving pleasure, to enjoy Daisy's body as well as making her happy, and to take her place physically as the receptacle for Craig's love. On Thanksgiving that year, I brought slices of turkey and buttered yams to the cabin for Daisy after our family dinner. While Craig and I feasted on each other, she feasted on the traditional food, eating and watching us with obvious relish, and then joined us for our communal climaxes.

It could be said that Craig and I shared Daisy, but Daisy and I shared Craig as well, as they shared me. Four lips dedicated to loving are better than two, I learned, and added variety to our love-making. And, as I reflected later, I learned that it was not necessary to reject roughly half the world's population as potential sex partners.

That fateful Sunday in early December was drizzly and cool. I was wishing for Craig, of course, but figured he would not venture out in this weather. I could envision Craig and Daisy, festooned on the large mattress in the hilltop cabin, with the fireplace a cozy companion. I would have liked to be there with them, basking in the glow of their friendship and sexuality. My thoughts were interrupted when Maria called to Dad and me from the kitchen where she was listening to the radio.

"The Japanese have attacked Pearl Harbor!" she gasped, and we crowded around the larger radio in the living room for the details as they became available, looking at each other helplessly. Our first reaction was anger for the people killed and ships destroyed in the sneak attack even while, we were told, the Japanese diplomats were making peaceful gestures in Washington. After the anger came anxiety over what this development would mean in our daily lives, the problems that now intruded in reality rather than the hypothetical that had operated until now.

"I don't think that farm deferment from the draft board will be effective now," Dad said sadly to me.

"I never wanted a deferment," I reminded him, seething with patriotic fervor of the moment. "I wish I could talk to Craig. We could go down to the induction center in the morning and enlist together!"

Dad looked at me and sighed, understanding better than I the implications. I thought only of my individual and our national resolve to fight back. Maria looked at both of us with teary eyes, feeling our conflicts. I knew she thought of me as nearly a son, since she had worked for the family since I was born.

Maria's husband had worked for my father for at least twenty years. He was well known to be a boozer, sometimes to be found passed out somewhere after several days' absence, but usually showed up for work and was a conscientious worker when sober. When I was born, Maria came to the main house to help my mother part-time during the day, and when my mother died of leukemia the previous year, she naturally became our full-time housekeeper. She had probably changed my diapers as many times as my mother, I assumed. She lived with her husband in a small house near the tool shed, behind the main house.

Dad looked at me with a questioning glance. "What about Louisa?" I guess I must have looked confused, but I knew immediately what he meant. Yes, what about Louisa? I had to face the issue I had been avoiding.

Just then the telephone rang; it was Louisa's father, Clarence; maybe telepathy was operating. He and my father had been close friends since childhood. Clarence had been my father's best man at my parents' wedding, and the families had remained close. Now they were coming to the house, apparently to confer on what the Pearl Harbor attack would mean for both families.

When they arrived the two fathers conferred alone in the kitchen while the rest of their family and I sat in the living room, subdued by the events and staring at each other. Louisa seemed more upset than I would have expected, and Sueann was very quiet with no trace of her usual provocative buoyancy. Louisa's mother was her usual stoic self, almost withdrawn it seemed to me. She rarely spoke.

The sun was breaking through, and I invited Louisa to take a walk like we used to do when we were younger. The deep blue California winter sky was a backdrop for the fragmenting cloud banks overhead. The grass along the roadside was already green from the earlier rains, growing through the golden remnants of summer.

We talked for a while about my plans, or lack of them, for military service. Her father was on the local draft board, and he had already told her that the draft would pick up now. There wouldn't be many young, single men left in the valley, now that we had been attacked. But I could tell there was something else on her mind in addition to the Pearl Harbor development. Eventually she came out with it.

"There's another problem that even my parents don't know about yet. It will have to remain a secret. Promise?"

"Sure, I guess so," I responded. She sighed heavily and blurted it out. "I'm quite sure Sueann is pregnant."

I blanched, but obviously Louisa didn't know completely why. My first thought was the scene at the Labor Day picnic — Craig's mighty orgasm while Sueann groaned and squealed her pleasure.

"Are you sure?" I persisted. "Pretty sure. Doctor Minton says she is probably about three months along." Her eyes were firmly fixed to the pavement and a blush highlighted her cheek bones that were already quite prominent. Sex and pregnancy were just not talked about, especially by such people as Louisa and her mother.

"Do you know, uh, who the father is?" She shook her head. "Sueann won't say, but you know how she is. She flirts with every man she meets, but I didn't know — I mean, I thought it was only an act, but I guess not." Was there a trace of irony in her voice?

Now I had to reach Craig for several reasons, but how? He probably didn't even know about the Pearl Harbor attack since he had no radio at his hilltop cabin. But Louisa was still talking.

"I sort of envy her in a way," she murmured. I stared at her, for the moment dumbfounded that she found anything fortunate about bearing an illegitimate child. In the Napa Valley in 1941, being pregnant without being married was just about the most horrific, socially unacceptable sin imaginable. Almost immediately, however, I grasped her meaning and felt anew the pangs of conscience my distraction from our youthful expectations had introduced. I also knew there was nothing I could do about it.

We returned to my house, my pace faster than Louisa wished. She was panting when we arrived. We found Craig sitting on his bike in the driveway, his face somber. I was so relieved to see him that I wanted to hug him, but of course resisted the temptation.

"I was at my parents' when the news came over the radio. What do you think?" he asked me, knowing I would understand his question.

At that moment Sueann came out of the house, heading for us with her usual coquettish smile for Craig. "Well, long time no see," she cooed at him. He merely smiled briefly and nodded "Hi," but returned to me. I noticed her eyes fixed on his face, perhaps remembering their previous meeting. I felt a stab of jealousy that was counteracted by the knowledge that I had experienced the same ecstasy and much more with Craig than she could ever imagine.

"I think we should enlist – tomorrow – together, I mean. What do you think?"

Sueann was tugging on Louisa's arm, drawing her away. I knew Louisa wanted to stay to hear our discussion, but Sueann was insistent. I was relieved to see them leave. They sat in the old porch swing suspended from the live oaks near the house, their heads together in sisterly conversation.

"If we went in together, do you think we could stay

together? Sort of like brothers, you know?" I asked him. I had never seen him look so grim. His green eyes were dark and his lips, usually seeming on the verge of smiling, were straight and set.

"I don't know. Which do you prefer? Army, Navy, or Marines?" he responded, obviously as determined but uncertain as I was. It was the kind of conversation that was going on throughout the country at that moment, we knew.

"Do we have a choice? Don't they just put us where they think there is the biggest need?"

"Hell, I don't know. I don't know much of anything these days," he growled. His obvious depression was something I hadn't seen before. Something had happened, something other than the Japanese attack on Pearl Harbor.

I longed to retreat with him to the mountaintop cabin, to lie with him, naked and close, where we shared our innermost secrets interspersed with kisses and caresses, our minds and bodies open and available to the other without thought of the intruding world around us. Daisy's silent presence was not inhibiting, and in fact rounded out the serenity. There were no unresolved issues between us, nothing forbidden or ignored. As frequently happened, Craig now sensed my question without my verbalizing it.

"Guess I'm grumpy, sorry. My Dad's been after me again about getting married and settling down, you know, and now this. . . "

"Yeah, well. . . Craig, I've got to talk to you. I − "

But then I began to rethink the situation. If we both went to the Army, perhaps the question of fatherhood of Sueann's baby would be avoided. If I told Craig that Sueann was pregnant, perhaps he would feel duty-bound to take responsibility. Maybe his father would actually take to the idea, satisfying his apparent anxiety to see Craig married, but what about us? I could feel the world, our

39

little valley world, suddenly and hugely magnified to extend across the Pacific and even to governmental Washington, DC. Those Japanese bombs were also destroying our utopia.

"I think we ought to enlist tomorrow, get it over with, as long as we can be together." I was ready to forget that I even knew about Sueann's problem. Craig looked at me in confusion, the brown flecks in his eyes darkening, and I could see that my urgency was contagious.

"What about Louisa? Are you going to marry her before you leave? And what about Daisy — who will take care of her?"

There was a moment of silence and then he muttered, "C'mon." I understood immediately, and silently agreed. He turned the bike around with a quick twist. I mounted the seat behind him and wrapped my arms around him; we sped off toward our cabin on the mountaintop, ignoring the startled faces of those behind us, stewing in family juices.

*   *   *   *   *   *   *

Louisa's account of what transpired after our departure was close to a Keystone Cop's episode, although Louisa was not noted for her sense of humor. Jaws dropped as we roared out of the driveway and disappeared down the highway. Then Sueann announced to her mother that she was pregnant, which started a loud gnashing of teeth and screaming denunciations between her parents. Then she told them tearfully that the father must be Craig, just as I had feared, although she glossed over the account of the actual event at the Labor Day picnic, to everyone's relief. Sueann's father, as head of the draft board, promised that, after Craig had made Sueann an honest woman, he would see to it that Craig was deferred from the draft so he could support his daughter in the manner he (the father) prescribed. I, of course, who might be expected to make trouble in one way or another, would be drafted promptly unless I married Louisa and settled down in wedded bliss as everyone had anticipated for many years. My father (reluctantly, I hope) agreed to this arrangement, probably figuring he had no choice, and by nightfall he was on the telephone to Craig's parents with the whole contrived plan.

Craig and I knew what was best for us, though. We knew what we needed was to be plugged into each other, literally as well as figuratively. Craig said it was called "69" but it was some time before I really understood the origin of that term. This time Daisy was not a part of the scene. It was a man's war, after all.

T here had been an overnight rain, but the skies were clearing rapidly that February morning when the families gathered to see me off for the Army. Mist was still wrapped around the scrub oak in the low lands when I drove the shiny Merc (for the last time) to the bus station. There was not enough breeze to clear the air of bus exhaust fumes from the loading lanes at the little depot.

Of course I had been roundly castigated by Louisa's family for refusing to go along with their scheme to marry her and thereby get a deferment. I think she understood when I told her that it wouldn't be fair to either of us since I wasn't really ready to get married, but there were tears and family squabbles. She had managed to enter the University in Berkeley in mid-term and seemed pretty enthusiastic about that. She didn't show up at the bus station, pleading a class conflict. That was OK with me.

Craig was there, of course, with Sueann, now showing pretty obviously and clinging to his arm. It had been a rough few weeks but Craig had accepted his fate, although he had managed to postpone the actual ceremony until I had gone (at my request). I couldn't bring myself to wish him good luck, knowing Sueann as I did and already having withdrawal symptoms from our separation. He had even managed to get Daisy into shoes for the occasion, although she hung back from the crowd, looking at me with her usual inscrutable, somber expression over their shoulders.

At nearly the last minute, some of the neighbors also showed up, thinking it was their patriotic duty to see one of their own going off to war. War feelings were high in the valley, and the few Japanese-American residents of the area were already encountering hostility from ordinary people they had known all their lives. Even Father Antonetti put in an appearance, striding into the little circle waiting at the bus stop with his usual glad-handing swagger. His wavy black hair and almost swarthy complexion were contrasts to most valley people who tended to be fair.

I happened to be looking at Daisy when the neighbors and the priest showed up. I had never seen such horror on a person's face; her expression was almost grotesque, her mouth was working, and then she darted out of sight, disappearing behind the drug store. She wasn't seen again for a long time.

I don't want to remember parting with Craig. I shook my father's hand and then hugged him loosely with properly controlled masculinity, ambivalent about how I really felt about him and his complicity in the recent turmoil. I tried to show the same restraint with Craig but I am sure, to anyone watching closely, I wasn't all that successful. I know there were tears in my eyes, but I didn't want even him to see them. We had said our more satisfying goodbyes the previous night, and I will never forget those intense hours in the little cabin. Those memories returned as solace on many nights in times to come.

("It shouldn't be too bad. They say the Army will make a man out of you," gripping me tightly with a calloused fist. "Haven't you already done that?" nibbling on his nipple. "God, if you become much more of a man, I won't be able to take this beautiful thing. . . ")

Only ten minutes late, the big gray bus with the bulldog on the hood headed south with me and a few north-bay business people. As we bounced along the country roads I reminded myself that this is what I had wanted, to serve my country in time of need, but somehow I had always included Craig in the picture. The rolling green hills with the rows of grape vines stretching up the slopes might never

43

look the same again, I thought, and I stored up those comforting images in my mind.

When we crossed the Golden Gate Bridge, the fog obscured the tops of the towers, but the view of the ocean to the west seemed unlimited. The city gleamed in the morning sun, accentuated by the clock tower of the Ferry Building. Across the Bay I thought I could make out the University campus in Berkeley, and wondered if Louisa was thinking about me at that moment. I still felt guilty about hurting her.

I had to change buses in San Francisco and there I encountered my first exposure to the Army. I had been instructed to report to a transfer sergeant. I had been concerned about finding him but he turned out to be quite obvious and very obviously in charge, barking contradictory orders at a growing group of raw recruits which I joined. By the time we boarded the bus for the trip to the southland, each man carrying big manila envelopes containing our orders, we were all completely confused about everything except that our lives were no longer our own. I guessed that was the main object.

We were all northern Californians but a mixture of rural or small town guys like me with some more sophisticated big-city guys who complained more loudly but were in actuality just as cowed by the sergeant's frustrated bluster. We didn't talk much on the trip, each harboring his own anxieties about what lay ahead. By late afternoon we were in basic training camp, lined up naked for physical examination, our clothes taken away to be shipped home. We all looked straight ahead of us, resisting the temptation to even glance below the other guys' waists in fear of being seized by military police and tortured or, worse, shipped home with our clothes on suspicion of being "queer."

When the bored and overworked doctor told us to bend over and spread our cheeks, at first I didn't understand what he meant. Then I wondered, for one heart-stopping moment, if he could tell just by looking that I had been fucked, royally and repeatedly, the night before. Either he couldn't tell or didn't care, since he said nothing.

The last step of the procedure was a private interview with a psychiatrist. His office, if that's what it was called, was a large, bare room that must have been intended for a classroom; he sat behind an old battered desk. He couldn't have been much older than I, or at least he was young and rather delicate looking, with dark, curly hair and spectacles. I still hadn't been issued any uniforms so was still naked and becoming chilled in the winter evening. The doctor gestured me in; he glanced at my face and then his eyes fixed on my crotch as I walked toward him across the bare, wood floor. I was acutely aware of my dick swinging against my thighs as I walked; it may even have grown a little from his intense scrutiny. I handed him my examination form as directed. He motioned me to sit on the cold metal folding chair in front of the desk, which made my balls shrivel when they made contact. At least his eyes returned to my face after I sat down.

He cleared his throat and asked what was obviously a standard question: "How do you think you will like the Army?"

How do you answer that kind of a question when you know you have no choice and need to make the best of it for as long as the war lasts? Of course I said, "Fine, sir." We had already been taught to add "Sir" to the end of every sentence because everybody in the world outranked us, and we really couldn't distinguish an officer from the lowest enlisted man from the uniform yet.

"Do you like girls?" His eyes seemed shaded, concealing his real thoughts. Maybe that's the way all psychiatrists were supposed to ask questions.

If I had been more comfortable in the situation and

45

permitted to be spontaneous, I would have laughed at the obvious question. Under the circumstances, however, we were treading on dangerous territory. I'm sure my eyes showed some of my ambivalence. I responded, "Sure."

"Do you have a girl friend back home?"

"Yes. Sir." I almost forgot to add the required word. I wondered briefly if Louisa would still be considered a "girl friend."

"How about boy friends?" Immediately his eyes dropped again toward my crotch, and a fantasy flashed across my brain, something involving the doctor, nude, kneeling between my feet, his lips opening in anticipation. . . I responded, "Yes. I mean, no sir." His eyes darted back to mine sharply. "You don't have any male friends?" I knew I was blushing but forced myself to continue. "Oh, yes, but − I mean, that's different. . . "

The doctor suddenly smiled, almost friendly. "Of course," he said soothingly. He scribbled something on my form and handed it to me. "I'm recommending you for the medics." I never discovered why he decided that I would be suited for the medical corps from those few short questions. Maybe they just needed medics that day.

I was directed out through another door and at last was issued some uniforms. Many of them did not fit properly; it was my first exposure to the impact that the haste of the country's mobilization after Pearl Harbor was having, but definitely not the last. With the entire group of recruits now dressed, we could at least associate with each other without reminding ourselves to keep our eyes up. We finally sat down to a meal, our first of the day, served by grumbling kitchen soldiers complaining about having to work late. I soon learned that complaining became an art and a recreation; if there was nothing new to complain about we dredged up some old infraction and reworked it.

46

At first it was exciting to be one of a large company of young men whose backgrounds and attitudes were different in detail but similar enough for companionship. My first few times in the shower with a half dozen guys, generally muscular and fit, all with appendages that swung with various degrees of authority, were sensual experiences. Eventually almost everyone grew erections for one reason or another. At first we would hide them if at all possible, but after a time no one seemed to notice or care. After a few days our overriding concern was fatigue and boredom; we were roused from our bunks at an ungodly early hour, forced to do calisthenics and race around the drill field before breakfast, attend classes on subjects that did not really interest us, and sometimes stand guard at night when we had to fight to keep our eyes open. We were repeatedly told that we, or rather our sacrificial bodies, were all that stood between life in the U.S. as we knew it and total destruction, annihilation at the hands of the crazed "Japs." Sex became a distant memory, something we could get along without.

Everyone masturbated, some more obviously than others, and in some cases there was a suggestion that masturbation was a form of display, of exhibitionism. It probably didn't mean that the guy was homosexual, but some others became disturbed by it, even to the point of complaining about it loudly. I never complained, but my masturbation fantasies about Craig were too special to make a show of it. When the double bunk was moving or squeaking so much from your bunk mate's activities that it was impossible to go to sleep, that was reason to complain.

There was one incident that departed from the routine. I was assigned in rotation to patrol the barracks of another company one night, from midnight to 4 AM. It was never clear just what the patrol was intended to accomplish, although we were told to watch for fires. Sixty men were

47

stacked two deep, that is, sleeping in double bunks. Although there were dim floor lights at intervals throughout the flimsy barracks, many of the bulbs had burned out and, like everything else, replacements were "backordered." At one end of that particular building, in the deep gloom of 2 AM, I noticed that the inhabitant of the upper bunk was sporting an erection. In itself that was not unusual, but in this case it was pointing to the side of the bunk, only inches away from me as I passed on my rounds. I dutifully paced to the opposite end of the building and returned, and this time I could discern the man's hand slowly stroking, and as I watched he moved even closer to the edge of the bunk, almost hanging off the bunk, closer to me. The man's face and most of his body was completely obscured in darkness.

Without thinking too much about it, I reached up to grasp the enticing rigidity and thrilled to its warmth and throbbing responsiveness. It wasn't Craig's, but it was hot and masculine and in need. I moved close to the bunk and took it into my mouth, hesitantly at first, and then more greedily as my own need reawakened. I heard the man's sharp intake of breath and a subtle groan as it moved into my throat. I allowed it to remain there for a moment as memories of Craig flooded my brain, a series of instant snapshots of our treasured moments.

I was not actually surprised when I felt fumbling at my fly, apparently from the lower bunk occupant, and my rigid cock exposed after some struggle. Quickly it was engulfed by what were probably inexperienced lips and mouth, and it was my turn to moan softly. Even a little scraping of teeth did not detract from the intense pleasure of that stolen moment. The bunk wobbled silently from the lower man's hand movements.

The entire episode really was little more than masturbation for all of us and was complete in probably about thirty seconds. There was no loving, no caresses, no promises for the future. I would not recognize either of my two sex partners if I bumped into them in the dining hall or on the drill field. But it was an acknowledgement that we were still humans with some individuality, appreciative of human subtlety, and not just cogs in a war machine as we were constantly being told by the U.S. Army.

C raig wrote that his wedding to Sueann, a quiet ceremony in the nave of the little village church, went off without a hitch. I wondered how Father Antonetti had rationalized the marriage with Sueann stretching a maternity dress, but the important thing had been accomplished. Craig had lived up to the community code, and the baby would have a name. He didn't say much about their personal relationship, and frankly I didn't ask or want to know. He also said that he had taken a P.O. box and I could write to him there without the letters falling into others' hands.

Apparently he had been thinking about what having a son would entail and, even though it should have happened otherwise, he was becoming quite enthusiastic about becoming a father. Never did he seem to consider that it might be a girl. A little boy to carry around on his shoulders, teach to ride a bicycle, help with his homework − those were the visions that Craig held in his inner world. I don't know whether he shared them with Sueann or not.

He also reported that Daisy had not reappeared since the day she fled the departure party at the bus station. He and Sueann were living in a small foreman's cottage behind his father's house, so the cabin on the top of the hill was empty. When he visited the cabin, there was no sign of Daisy. Since he did not know where she had come from originally, there was no way to trace her.

Army basic training, thankfully, was of short duration, accelerated, they said, because they needed us in the field (as cannon fodder, it was assumed). However, true to his word, the psychiatrist had put my name on the medic school list and so, with very little fuss, I simply moved to another building on the base and started my "specialty" training.

We had more free time and the days were spent in more intellectual pursuits, which suited me. We had to learn the names of all the bones of the body and the names and locations of all the blood vessels so we could put pressure on the correct areas to arrest bleeding in casualties. There was some attention paid to use of drugs, but it was obvious that our main function was first aid and transporting the wounded. When faced with an open wound, our first act should be to dust sulfa powder into it and get the patient to a doctor.

For the first time since I left home I went into town on a weekend pass. The USO groups were becoming organized and canteens were set up outside the major bases to entertain the troops. The presence of hostesses was a welcome change for me. It seemed sometimes that if I ever smelled another man's armpits it would be too soon, and yet I knew the sexual attraction was still there, dormant, needing little to reawaken it. The perfumed world of crinolined women beckoned.

Most of the hostesses were ordinary girls who needed some excitement in their lives; most of them were somewhat frightened of the men while desiring their company at the same time. Maybe Louisa wasn't unusual. I wondered sometimes how she would react in this situation, but the question was academic. Dancing was the usual mechanism for getting to know the hostesses, although that particular exercise had never been particularly attractive to me in high school. After hesitating the first few times, sipping my beer at the bar and watching the festivities while screwing up my courage, I gradually blended into the picture of the lonesome GI out on the town, needing female companionship. Of course among our buddies we also characterized ourselves, more or less, to be predatory studs out to "dip our wick" wherever we could get away with it. We weren't looking for wives.

In retrospect, the hasty episode with the two guys in the barracks probably was responsible for allowing me the mental freedom to indulge my sexuality. For weeks after my induction, my sexual fantasies were largely related to Craig, although Daisy was included in those memories. When I awoke with a hardon, which was practically every morning, I thought of Craig and what we would do about it, or with it, or with his. . . The incident in the barracks awoke the realities that there were others with whom to have sex, satisfying sex, uncomplicated and without profound consequences. I just had to learn how to be a "stud" like other men, or at least like other GIs far from home.

Carole was my first dance partner of consequence. She was a pugnosed blond, so short that she came barely to my nipples, but she plastered herself to me from the start and gave me a hardon within seconds after taking her into my arms. She excused herself after one dance, choosing another GI, but I noticed she also extracted herself from him after one dance and went on to another. All evening she changed partners after brief forays, leaving every man with erections but no one satisfied. Burt, with whom I had struck up a conversation, called her a "prick teaser," and I guess he was correct.

I had seen Burt around the base and after chatting for a while at the bar was impressed with his friendly sophistication. He was a tall, rangy Irishman with characteristic black hair and dancing blue eyes. He had a trace of an accent, since his parents had brought him to the U.S. when he was a youngster. He said he was from Noe Valley, and it was some time before I learned that that was a neighborhood in San Francisco near Mission Street. He was attending an engineering school at the base. Picking up

52

girls had been a hobby of his for several years, apparently, but he said he preferred dark-haired Latinas of a type rare in the region of the base. He danced at least once with every girl in the place.

Laura was a little shy, and maybe that's why we hit it off. She had recently graduated from high school and had moved away from her home in the country to work in a defense plant that was just going into production. I admired her courage and also her breasts that set my own nipples on "tilt" when we danced. Her hair was rather mousey but her dark eyes and rosebud lips made up for minor defects. She shared a small apartment with another girl who worked the swing shift, and after our second date we were able to go to her apartment and have rather rushed sex in a narrow, rollaway bed. My experiences with Daisy had not prepared me very well, it seemed, because Laura was hesitant where Daisy had been forthright, appeared almost shocked where Daisy had smiled invitingly, and she seemed in a rush to clean up afterwards. I hadn't learned how to postpone my climax under such conditions, but when we were able to repeat the next week it worked out better.

Laura did not appear the following week, but I met Joanne, a flashy brunette who seemed to love to play with my hair. There wasn't much of it, of course, after the GI barbers were finished, but she said she liked blonds. I had a flashback of an evening on the shore of the lake back home, Craig smiling down at me and saying "I have a thing for blonds. . .," but I shoved that memory back into a secret recess reserved for him. Burt was also interested in Joanne, but she made it very clear that I had the inside track with her. Burt winked at me goodnaturedly and walked away to continue his search. With some guys that could have started an argument, but not Burt. I never saw him become upset or be unkind to anybody. Joanne had a car and, while that was never my preferred theater of operations, we made do. She was unusually athletic and seemed to love oral sex, although she was not very expert, it seemed to me. She said she loved the blond hair in my crotch, too.

Spring had come and the days were heating up regularly. The evenings didn't cool down as much as I was used to in the Napa Valley. There were fans in the barracks and the windows were left open, but sleeping was still troublesome. No one slept with more than a sheet over them, and usually that was kicked off before morning. The rows of double bunks down both sides of the narrow building looked like a forest of short, throbbing trees at night; we all had towering hardons and no one seemed to think anything of it, except me, of course. Even I was getting accustomed to the constant masculine sensuality almost to the point of losing its fascination. Our only outlet, other than masturbation, was the Saturday night dances.

Of course I made friends with many of the guys who attended the dances, too. When I felt I didn't need to study for the next day's classes, the base Canteen became the center of social life in the evening. Some of us "veterans" of the Saturday night dances met there and swapped stories about the previous week's conquests. Burt and I frequently drank beer together in the Canteen and also at the dances, commiserating when our little affairs didn't work out and celebrating when they did. Much of the time the problem in "making out" was a place to go for sex. One night a girl and I tried it standing up in a dark alley behind some garbage cans and I ending up jacking off anyway, with my arm around the girl. I don't think she got much out of it, and that was also disturbing.

One day Burt suggested that we rent a cheap room at one of the local hotels for the night. That way we had a place to go, and we could afford it by splitting the cost. The next week we were more confident as we surveyed the "crop," but it turned out that I didn't score that night and he had the room all to himself. That was OK – *c'est la guerre*; we were accustomed by this time to events being under the control of others, including the U.S. Army and Lady Luck.

We rented a room the next weekend, also. Joanne was there again, flirting with me and ignoring Burt, but I had an idea. I checked it out with Joanne first, who was always ready to try something new, or so she said. I then proposed to Burt that we make it a three-way in the hotel room. He knew it was the only way he would ever get close to Joanne, and agreed without much hesitation. He also mentioned that he had an extra condom in case I didn't have any. I looked confused, and he was shocked to hear that I had never used them. "Some of these girls would like nothing better than to get pregnant and get our monthly allotment check," he muttered in my ear. "To say nothing about our getting V.D." As I said, he was sophisticated.

We were all a little drunk when we arrived at the hotel. Joanne had brought us in her car, and it weaved rather obviously from time to time as it wound through the narrow streets. The room had one double bed (it would have cost more with an extra bed) and one easy chair, so there wasn't much choice about where the action was. Even with the light off, the room was illuminated by the big red hotel sign outside. I immediately took her in my arms, something I couldn't do properly in her car, and she responded warmly for a moment, then looked over my shoulder at Burt. Hesitantly he came alongside, and she included him in our embrace. I could tell he didn't know what to do with me, but finally we ended up in a three-way embrace and we all grinned at each other, pleased with being a little naughty.

We separated and she began to undress. Burt also started stripping everything off. I had never seen such speed in divesting clothing, but before Joanne had her dress off, he was nude. He told me later he always liked to watch

55

the girls undress, unhampered by his own disrobing. He was an amazing specimen, big and muscular, a thick nest of black hair in the middle of his broad chest, and a very large cock not yet fully erect. What caught my attention was his foreskin, extending at least an inch beyond his cock head. I had had no experience with an uncircumcised cock, and particularly not one so big. Where I was born and raised, every boy was circumcised soon after birth; it was such an accepted practice that I had never seen a cock that wasn't cut until I joined the Army. Joanne merely glanced at it and returned to watching me, although I was much slower at undressing than Burt.

We were soon in very much of a *ménage à trois*, and I was in my element. I won't go through all the permutations, but at one point, Burt, always courteous, was signaling me to enter her as he waited alongside. He already was sheathed in his condom, and he handed another one to me. I fumbled with it, having no experience – probably had it upside down. Quickly, with no hesitation, he took my cock in one hand and deftly fitted the condom over it, rolling it down effortlessly and rapidly, anxious to get on with it. I could tell that he thought there was nothing special about holding my cock while he applied the condom, but I don't think I had ever had as rigid a cock as when his fist was around it.

Joanne was in her element. Everywhere she turned she had some part of masculine anatomy to do with as she wished. I knew exactly what she was experiencing, although my own role in this little group was much more restricted than it had been in the little cabin on the hill. I think I taught Burt a few tricks about three-ways that night, and I hoped there would be more opportunities.

It seemed strange for the girl to leave, driving her own car, with the two of us left behind. We all laughed about it and off she went, and to the shower we went, one at a time, of course. Before turning off the light, Burt thanked me for "being such a good sport," sharing my date with Joanne that way. Then he said he hoped there was room for me in the bed, because he was such a big "galloot," I think was his expression. Of course I graciously accepted his gratitude and the apology for his bulk. I didn't sleep much that night, but at least I had some new fantasies to roll out when the time was right.

7

I thought perhaps Burt would regret sharing the room, but he made the hotel reservations the next week without even asking me. The temperature had soared even higher, and the standard uniforms were much too heavy for the weather. We were not allowed to wear anything but our uniforms, even when off the base. Theoretically we could be recalled at any moment in case of some catastrophe.

The newly-organized USO had managed to install some air conditioners for the dance, but they were inadequate to the task. It wasn't comfortable to dance, to hold a warm body in your arms, and most people just sat at tables or the bar with iced drinks. In spite of the conditions, Burt came up to me and introduced a girl named Gloria, a brassy type with dark hair coiled on top of her head and wearing a dress with a neckline nearing her navel. "Gloria says she wouldn't mind getting to know two soldiers rather than just one tonight," Burt explained, more than a little inebriated. "You game?"

"Sure!" I agreed. She wasn't the type I would choose, but there were obvious compensations. We took a cab to the hotel and had to climb three flights of stairs to the room because the elevator had broken down. We were all dripping wet when we arrived, and opening the window did little to cool the air.

"OK," I proclaimed, "everybody in the showers!"

Gloria squealed and agreed that was a good idea. Soon the three of us had crowded nude into the bathtub around which a stained linen curtain was drawn, trying to sluice off the perspiration and cool off. It worked to a degree, but of course it became a "let's both feel up Gloria" session. I had to remind myself repeatedly not to touch Burt in an obvious way, but it was fun. None of us was really cool when we moved to the bed.

Gloria turned out to be almost as worldly as she seemed. This time she helped me put on the condom, although it had been more exciting with Burt. I noticed, as I was doing my thing between her legs, that she was attempting to take Burt orally but without much success. Burt was trying to cooperate, even whispering instructions to her on the finer points, but they obviously didn't have much luck. A comparison of his thick cock with her tiny mouth was warning enough, and there was the added factor of the foreskin.

By the time we finished, we were all soaking wet again and the towels were still wet from the previous shower, so we sat around naked in the slight breeze through the window until we had dried off somewhat. We tried to make intelligent conversation but Gloria was just not up to it, unfortunately. Eventually, after several pointed suggestions, she got dressed and we arranged for a cab to take her home. When she had finally gone, Burt and I looked at each other and burst into laughter about the crazy situation.

We both rolled into bed, still chuckling, and I turned the light out. "No sheet tonight," he mumbled, stretching his long legs out, nude and hairy. Then he chuckled again. "Sex is never bad, you know, only better some times than others." We went into another laughing jag and then gradually settled down again. The red light shining in the window seemed to make the room even warmer than it was. I waited for a couple of minutes before I asked my question.

"You were hoping she would suck you off, weren't you?"

"Yeah, I was hoping. But girls just don't seem to

understand — I mean they just can't seem to handle it — can't blame them, I guess."

"You mean — your foreskin?"

"Yeah, that seems to be a problem. I try to teach them but it just doesn't seem to work out — "

A few more moments of silence passed before I asked the important question. "Want to teach me?"

"Oh! I didn't mean — I wasn't expecting — you mean, you want to?"

"Yeah."

"Well, yeah, sure, if you want to. . . "

I moved down and lifted his thick, soft cock with a trembling hand. He began his instructions. I paid close attention and I did what he told me to do, trying to appear as if it was completely new to me.

"See, it's best to start with it soft, like it is now. You put your tongue in the folds and sort of snake it in the soft tunnel-like, ah, yeah, like that, yeah — and you move your tongue around, sort of pushing inward — ah — Of course I start getting hard, you know, so then you try to get your tongue in between the loose skin and the head — oh, shit — and you run it around the head — uh — yeah — uh — you keep doing that and doing that until I can't stand it anymore — " His voice was rising and his cock was growing, getting very hard; mine was already bursting at the seams. "And then pull the skin back to push the head out, exposing the whole thing — Christ, yeah! — and lick around the head a little — Christ, yeah! — yeah — and you go down, way down — shit, man, oh shit — taking it all if you can — oh, yeah, yeah — until I can feel it all the way down your throat, the bare head, I mean, and you suck it — oh, yeah — suck it up and down, your tongue lapping and your lips tight around the shaft — oh, God, suck it — suck it — take the head all the way down — suck it — Matt!

Matt, I'm going to − you better stop − "

He would have to fight me off to get me to stop. If I hadn't had my mouth full I would have told him that. He didn't fight. Although we had both climaxed earlier with Gloria, I am sure the second time was better, for both of us, even though mine was in my hand.

When we had both caught our breaths again, we lay back, looking at the cracked ceiling. "So good," he sighed. "You're a real buddy." After a moment he turned on his side and was asleep in less than a minute. Burt was the most uncomplicated guy I had ever met. In spite of the heat, I slept like a log.

Our search for sex partners was simpler after that night. When one of us would seem to find a worthy partner, and assuming the girl was agreeable (most were), it would be a three-way at the hotel. During sex the following week, I managed to share his cock surreptitiously with a girl while he was occupied between her legs. She was startled by my trickery, but then smiled as a collaborator in my little secret.

After she had gone we went to bed. I always looked forward to going to sleep with him, our butts touching as if by accident. I closed my eyes and was drifting off but I was startled awake when Burt murmured, "That was you sucking my dick for awhile tonight, wasn't it?" "Yep." A moment of silence. "Want to try it again?" "Yep."

Occasionally we would both strike out − we called it "famine" when the supply of agreeable hostesses would dry up for some reason. It really wasn't much of a problem; I welcomed the opportunity to take both his first and second loads. He never touched me in any truly sexual way, but that didn't matter. That wasn't his nature and it was mine, it was as simple as that. We were best friends and I never wanted or expected more.

B urt graduated and was sent off to some Pacific base. I hated to see him go but I also graduated two weeks later, after which I had a furlough before being sent to my next duty station. I returned home on July 1; my father met me at the bus station.

He looked older than I remembered and the home town seemed smaller, more rustic. I felt almost a stranger, but I looked forward to shedding my drab uniform and returning to some old, comfortable civilian clothes for a change. The '39 Merc was gone. Craig had bought it, Dad explained, and it had been replaced by a new Ford, probably the last model to be released until the war was over.

"How is Craig?" I asked on the way home. His occasional letters had seemed to grow cooler in tone while I was away, but I thought it was because he wasn't used to communicating in that manner. I had hoped he would be at the station to meet me when I arrived.

"Oh, yeah, I meant to tell you. I heard that Craig and Sueann's baby was born last night. I'm sure he'll want to tell you all about it."

Maria gave me a big hug when we arrived home, and there were tears in her eyes. She served a big Mexican lunch, including all the special dishes I used to ask for, but I didn't tell her that I had really grown tired of the bad Mexican food served at the Canteen and would have preferred something else.

We had just finished lunch when the phone rang. It was Craig and I rushed to the phone, hungry for him, but he sounded like any other friend might, welcoming a service man home from the Army. He was probably calling from his parents' house, I reasoned, and so had to be cautious about his enthusiasm. He suggested we meet at the hospital during viewing times so I could see his new–born son.

We were both shy with each other when we met at the hospital in Santa Rosa. He looked as sexy as ever – or almost; there seemed to be a line between his eyes that wasn't there before. His mouth no longer held that trace of a grin that had always intrigued me, waiting for the blossoming of his wit, the punchline of a joke. Perhaps I also looked older and more experienced to him, he didn't say. Then the nurse brought the baby for us to see at the window, and my jaw dropped.

He was a beautiful baby – with unusually long coal-black hair and pale olive-brown skin. It was difficult to match his features with either Craig, with his blond-brown hair, green eyes, and fair skin, or Sueann, blue eyed and blond from top to toe. I tried to be enthusiastic, congratulating him with a masculine hug, but I had some doubts. Did he? I didn't want to bring it up. At least his dreams of a boy to love and raise had come true, and I was happy for him on that score.

"Isn't he beautiful?" he sighed, pressing against the glass window. "I can't wait for him to walk and talk and toddle after me in the vineyards. . ." The vineyards. They already seemed strange and far away to me, although we were in the heart of the wine country, my birthplace. I was beginning to realize the profound effects of a few months away from home, and the way the war was changing people and things, forever. "And Sueann will be a good mother, too, just wait and see," he continued. Apparently he was still able to read my mind.

Explaining that the baby would be taken soon to Sueann for nursing and he wanted to wait around for that, we went to the coffee shop to chat. He wanted to hear all about my experiences in the Army, but when I started to mention sexual episodes with men he grew uneasy, looking around for eavesdroppers, and changed the subject. Over coffee I asked him about married life, and he seemed somewhat cautious and superficial, as though he was telling me what he wanted to be known generally.

"Dad says next spring he will build another room onto the foreman's cottage for the baby. Sueann's pretty cramped there, and it will be worse with the baby, of course. Did your Dad tell you I bought the '39 Merc, your pride and joy? She and I even made out a little once at the drive-in theater before she got too far along, and I remembered. . . " His voice tapered off, almost as if he didn't want to remember the times when we had steamed up the windows because there was no other convenient place to go to have sex.

"Maybe we could get together in your cottage before Sueann comes home from the hospital?" I suggested. I was confident that once I got him in bed all the changes would disappear and he would again be the sexy, masculine idol I kept in my hidden memory recess.

He shifted uneasily, looking away. "Well, maybe. . . we ought to talk about that." I'm sure he saw the disappointment in my face, but he looked at his watch then and said we should go to see Sueann.

When we walked into Sueann's room she already had company. Father Paul Antonetti was there in all his sanctified aura, his Tyrone Power–handsome, Bing Crosby–phony priesthood (if you can imagine a glamorously-masculine, swash-buckling priest in "Bells of St. Mary's"). As we entered he was stroking Sueann's forehead gently while she nursed the baby somewhat awkwardly. He broke contact as soon as he saw us, making me wonder if it was only a pastoral gesture. We shook hands and I tried to seem friendly. Sueann looked flushed, but I guessed that that was an expected part of the post-pregnancy period. Maybe she was embarrassed for me to see her nursing the baby at her breast, which was certainly larger than I had expected. Craig seemed to ignore the priest and, after a peck of Sueann's cheek, was absorbed in admiring the baby.

We chatted for a while until the baby had stopped nursing. Father Antonetti asked if he could hold the baby; he picked him up and held him against his chest, and I almost gasped. The resemblance between them was striking. I was pretty sure I understood the situation then. I also knew I had to keep it to myself unless the subject came up in another way.

When the nurse came for the baby, we left. On the way out, Craig asked if I would be the godfather. I said, sure. "I'll ask Sueann about using 'Matthew' as his middle name. She wants 'Paul' for the first name."

"Paul? Why Paul?"

"After some grandfather or something, I guess. Somebody I don't know. It's as good as any, I guess."

"I see." And I was pretty sure I did.

"By the way," I interjected. "As the godfather I guess I have some say about little — Paul. I don't think he should be circumcised. Is that OK with you?"

Craig stopped short at the door of the old Merc, looking at me blankly. He had obviously not thought about it. "Why?" he asked.

I grinned a little mischievously at him. "Well, I've had some experience with foreskins, and they can be really fun, you know? And I think he'll appreciate it when he gets old enough to understand."

Craig looked away, his jaw tight. "Gees, Matt, he's only one day old and you're talking about his getting his cock sucked. He's not going to be a pansy! I'm going to see to

65

that — bring him up right, I mean, to stick to girls."

I stared at him, my memories of him in disarray. Was this the man who, only nine months ago, explained to me how everybody was born bisexual and having sex with guys was only one normal function of living? That "triple plays" were frosting on the cake to sexual relationships with either gender? He was a stranger to me. My love was withering like grape leaves after the frost.

"About your coming over to the cottage — I don't think it's a good idea, Matt. I know what you want, and I used to want it, too, you know that. But since Sueann and I got married I've been faithful, and I'm going to stay that way. I owe it to the baby." He looked out toward the golden hills, his face set determinedly. The thought crossed my mind that if it required this much effort to be "normal," why did he bother? If this is what marriage did for you —

"But sure, if you don't want Paul to be circumcised, I'll tell the doctor not to do it. It's OK."

I didn't understand how having sex with me would somehow jeopardize his vow to be faithful to Sueann. I wasn't another woman, so how could it be considered being "unfaithful?" I had the impression that if I could get him into bed, naked in my arms, that his erection would be as firm as ever and I could talk some sense into his head, but from his expression I knew his mind was made up for the present, at least. I turned to walk away, disheartened. This furlough was not going to be the paradise I had dreamed of.

"Oh, by the way," Craig continued from behind me, "how about bringing Louisa around after Sueann leaves the hospital? Maybe we could go out for dinner or something, if my mother will baby-sit for us."

"Yeah, OK," I answered shortly over my shoulder. I had to get away, to think this out.

66

Louisa. I hadn't given much thought to her.

I called her that evening. She also sounded a little cool, but busy with her college course work, she said. I mentioned Craig's suggestion about double-dating after Sueann was discharged from the hospital, and she was hesitant. Finally she suggested having coffee with me at a downtown coffee shop, which was pretty unusual, I thought. I didn't sleep much that night, going over in my mind the last few months I had spent at home before entering the Army, but the following day I was sitting at the marbleized formica table in the little coffee shop when she arrived.

She hadn't changed much, I thought, not as much as everyone else. The afternoon was hot with the sun blasting down, but I wasn't feeling very sunny. She smiled at me, complimenting me on how well I looked, how handsome I was in the uniform. I had heard it all before.

The conversation seemed more superficial than it used to be between us. Finally she sighed, looked around to make sure she could not be overheard, and then explained her hesitation about the date.

"I'm sure this will come as a shock to you," she began, looking down at her untouched cup of coffee. "Attending classes in Berkeley has opened my eyes to so many new things — I never realized how primitive we were here in the Napa Valley, although San Francisco and Berkeley are so close."

I nodded, but she continued, still looking away.

"You see — I met a friend in Berkeley — a girl — and discovered that I — well, I really like her and — and we had sex. . . I guess I am a lesbian."

While I was surprised, it all seemed to make more sense now. We had both been trying to fit the mold that others had designed for us, but neither was of the appropriate material. But there was still the question: "But why not both?"

She stared at me, puzzled. "But — I told you — I prefer sex with women! We understand each other instinctively, want the same things, and when she touches me — " The assumption was that the situation was black and white.

What was going on here? First Craig swore off sex with men (and other women) because he got married, as uncertain as that linkage may be, and then Louisa couldn't imagine sex with men just because she liked sex with women! Was I the only one who could go both ways, enjoy both men and women sexually for their natures and their attributes, without some major block? I was becoming more and more confused. Of course the fact remained that if Louisa felt nothing for men, there was nothing to be gained by discussing it. I resolved to try once more.

"Are you repulsed by the idea of having sex with a man?"

She blushed and looked even more dejected. "Well — not really, I suppose — but — well, I'm just not interested." I also got the idea that her friend, or lover or whatever she was, would be unhappy if Louisa strayed from the fold.

We separated to go home, both of us probably more confused about our sexuality than when we were "going steady" in high school. I started the new Ford, still fragrant with that new car smell, but I would have preferred the old, comfortable Merc. Everything was changing around me. My life as I thought I knew it was no longer. For some reason Louisa's confession seemed like another desertion, abandonment adding to Craig's betrayal of our relationship, and the highway swam before my eyes as I drove toward home. Impulsively, instead of taking the highway home, I sped past the turnoff, straight for the lake where it had all begun with Craig.

There were no cars in the parking lot, only a few

bicycles belonging to kids splashing in the muddy water, trying to cool off. Without thinking I started off at a near run up the wooded path toward the crest of the hill. I had to think, and the best place I could think of for that was at the hilltop. The dust skittered under my feet as I dashed upward; I scrambled over outcropping rocks, stumbled over exposed roots of the towering eucalyptus, the sweat beginning to trickle down my chest. Impatiently I threw my cap to the side of the path and a moment later stripped off my shirt and tie, leaving them behind alongside the path. Still I climbed, my breath labored, and soon my pants were also left behind. I was just past the half-way point when I tore off my sodden undershirt and shorts, climbing the rest of the way completely bare except for my shoes. At last I stood at the summit, naked and breathless, the valley spread out before me, green rows of vines alternating with golden fields of dry grass under the pale blue, summer sky. And to my left hunkered the tiny cabin where we had spent so many hours making love. It was the proper place to bring my pain.

The door was slightly ajar but the interior was dim and appeared undisturbed. The bed in front of the fireplace was neatly made as if waiting for me. I slumped to its comforting coolness and stared at the rough ceiling that had shaded our private moments. I suddenly realized that I was erect, and I grasped myself tightly, as if my only grip on reality. Anytime now Craig would come in, wearing that infectious grin that meant he wanted me as much as I wanted him, but my eyes clouded because I knew he wouldn't. My tears dimmed the emptiness around me but my cock was rigid, waiting. I relived that Sunday afternoon when Craig was in my arms and he was thick and sweet in my mouth. . .

I became aware of a shadow at the door and looked up. A young women, barely more than a girl, barefoot and wearing a limp cotton house dress, stood in the doorway, blinking into the dimness of the cabin. She entered with a peculiar, gliding gait, almost catlike. She began to dance slowly, sinuously, to music only in her head. Suddenly she whipped her dress off over her head, still dancing, and then floated to me on the mattress. She lowered herself over me, fitting me into her living warmth, embracing my potency, sheltering me from the darkness that threatened to consume me. She began to move slowly, languorously, her head thrown back and her breasts pointing upward and − almost immediately I convulsed, thrusting upward, silently screaming. The flow of passion was at first tumultuous, roiling, frothing waves breaking over us, but then moments later, as the tide ebbed, I realized that the festering torment had been drained, my fever cooled, leaving me spent but relieved of much of the grief that had brought me there.

Daisy's long, black hair soothed my face as I closed my eyes and slept.

The temperature wasn't much different in Washington D.C. than I was used to in the Napa Valley, but the humidity, hovering around 90%, was new and denervating. When the bus turned into the long drive of Walter Reed Army Hospital and the extensive buildings and rolling, grassy campus came into view, I wondered if there was some mistake. Army bases were supposed to be sterile, dusty flatlands not good for anything else, weren't they?

And when I lugged my meager possessions to the barracks assigned to me, I was in for another surprise. My spacious two-story masonry address had gleaming waxed floors (which I was not responsible for cleaning and waxing), wide halls, and dormitory rooms with only twenty beds (not double-deckers). Walls about seven feet high divided two-man cubicles from each other, with a central aisle containing full-height lockers that formed partial separations from traffic. They were almost semi-private rooms, except for the open view of the cubicle on the other side of the central aisle. I collapsed on my assigned bed, which even had real sheets and plump pillows, feeling like a millionaire in khaki.

I had barely finished hanging up my uniforms in the spacious locker when my "room mate" arrived, giving me a quiet but friendly hello. He shucked his cap and some files he was carrying in his locker and then headed for the latrine, so I didn't get a good look at him until he returned. The unaccustomed semi-privacy was only as comfortable as was the relationship with one's room mate, I realized.

Wes North was several years older and a sergeant, several grade levels higher in rank than I, but then I was almost at the lowest end of the totem pole at that point. He looked like one of those people who was always on the upper side of the slope from sheer energy and knowledge, but I soon learned that he was entirely free of illusions and bravado. His blue eyes sparkled good naturedly at me, but were basically serious and contemplative. A nascent line on each side of his mouth seemed to suggest that he had experienced pain but it had not discouraged him. He rarely initiated a conversation, but responded quickly when I did. I liked him from the start.

"This is sure different from my last duty station," I sighed.

"Just out of medic school?" he asked with a kind rather than supercilious tone as most guys would have. His voice was soft, almost feminine, but with a crisp edge.

"Yeah," I smiled. "West coast. I'm from Napa." I could see I had stumped him for a minute. "Napa?" I grinned. "Yeah, just north of San Francisco. Wine country." "Oh, yeah," he said, looking away. He seemed to be storing up the information in his brain to be retrieved accurately some time in the future. He stretched out on his bed, hands behind his head, which apparently was his favorite position.

"You?"

"Oh, here and there. Army brat. Moved a lot. Born in Panama." His speech was consistently produced in snatches, giving only the salient words with few modifiers. I found it soothing after the loudmouthed, garrulous nitwits that I had frequently encountered in the Army. I also found myself using the same abbreviated form of communication frequently when we conversed. When I stretched out on my bed, only a few feet from him, the silence was companionable.

My stomach growled; I had had nothing to eat for what seemed like days. "Where's the mess hall?" I asked.

He immediately rose and retrieved his cap. "I'll show you." On the way he pointed out some features of the campus that I would need to know to get around. The food was also much better than the semi-solid, sometimes unidentifiable slop I had become used to in Basic.

"You starting school?" he asked during the meal.

"Yeah, surgery technician course," I answered.

"Oh yeah, fattening you up for the kill, eh?" I looked at him questioningly.

"You must be considered top grade," he explained. "The best and brightest of the students in primary school are usually sent here to train in surgical techniques so they can run aid stations just behind the front lines – doing triage and emergency procedures. The enemy artillery delights in picking them off. Highest mortality rate of any medic group, they say." It was a long speech for Wes.

"I don't know," I responded uncertainly. I had considered I was lucky to be going to a special school, and the prospect of that kind of assignment excited me agreeably. I thought again about the strange doctor who had initially decided I should become a medic, wondering what he had detected about me that I was unaware of myself.

"What do you do?" I asked him, a rather strange question, I knew, in this highly specialized corps.

He didn't answer directly. "Oh, I am also in training, sort of. It's classified." He never provided a clear picture of his assignment, but I learned that he spent most of his time in the Administration building where all the upper brass were assigned, and he was quite protective of the files he seemed to carry with him at all times during the day. There was even a special locked compartment in his locker, I discovered later.

There was one disadvantage in this new, relatively palatial environment, I discovered, when we returned to the

73

barracks and I decided to shower. The huge, communal showers standard in basic training, usually occupied by a half-dozen guys soaping up and eyeing each other, were replaced by individual shower stalls that had a linen curtain. There would be no more subtle teasing in the shower. Of course it was also easier to masturbate behind the curtain, I thought immediately, and I proceeded to prove that point as a sort of initiation ceremony. It wasn't much fun, but it relieved the tension.

Most of the guys in the dorm spent much of the time wearing towels wrapped around their waists, either getting ready for or having just finished a shower. Wes never was that informal. He always wore regulation shorts when relaxing, and even wore them when walking to the shower. I followed him into the latrine a few times, but saw no more than a very trim ass as he slipped into the shower stall, hanging his towel and shorts on hooks just outside. His body was almost hairless but well muscled, without an ounce of excess fat. Many of the other guys in the dorm were much sexier and even sometimes flirtatious, but I never saw Wes looking at another guy or acknowledging anyone's interest in him. For me his isolated mannerisms made him sexier. The lure of the unknown, I suppose. Of course it was even more important to remain "chaste" in this more advanced cadre, I realized.

My course at Walter Reed was indeed specialized and more challenging than I had experienced before. It consisted partially of lectures from doctors who were specialists in their fields, plus experience on surgical wards. But much of our time was spent in surgery, learning sterile techniques and surgical assistant skills, "scrubbing" and "circulating," which were terms for those assisting the doctors at the operating table and those free to assist in the room from behind the operating team respectively. Part of these duties involved "prepping" the operative area by scrubbing with special solutions and in predetermined sequence of maneuvers to obtain optimal sterility. It was there that we were the most closely supervised and most frequently found wanting.

The other guys in my class were a mixture of obviously bright intellects plus a few oddballs. In particular I noticed a strange little guy from New Orleans called Claude Marcel. Every day his hair was done in a different mode; one day it was drooped down over one eye, unsuccessfully imitating the movie actress, Veronica Lake, I thought. He explained that, now that we were allowed to have more than the closest of crew cuts, he was exploring various styles to see which one he liked best. That seemed pretty strange, but I had never met anyone from New Orleans, so maybe he wasn't so strange after all. He spoke with a really peculiar accent, I thought. I could tell he had a good body but I never saw much of it when we changed into scrub suits. Because he was so flamboyant, I decided not to become too friendly with him, although I liked him. Craig had used the expression "let his hair down," which indicated being obvious about being queer. Maybe that was what Claude was actually doing in his own, comical way.

Our direct superiors were nurses who were generally tyrants, apparently relishing the opportunity to oversee young men, snapping at us for minor infractions and drilling us in the finest details of sterile technique. Some of them outranked many of the doctors, but there was no question that the doctors' words were law when it came to patient care regardless of Army rank. The doctors taught us anatomy first hand as they operated, frequently with a fatherly but somewhat militaristic attitude, knowing better than we what we might encounter in the field when we had finished our training. We admired them greatly, and sometimes conspired with them against the nurses when we could.

There was only one right way to do everything, each maneuver peculiar to the instrument and usage. To drop something would bring down unimaginable abuses from the nurses, especially Miss Milsted, the head nurse. She pretended that even the tiniest mistake by a medic would bring upon her head the castigation of the entire medical profession, and of course she could do no wrong. The younger nurses were more permissive, but she was almost as tyrannical with them as with the enlisted men.

Some of the younger doctors were conscripts like us, but since they were officers they could get by with more blunders or bending of the rules. Dr. Corey was one of my favorites. I suspected that he was "one of us" in private life; occasionally he would make slips that were only half unintentional. My eyes met his many times in various situations, where we secretly shared some minor amusement at some silliness. I was beginning to think I could spot other men with queer tendencies, and I was sure he was "one." I suspected that, on the "outside," we might have hit it off, but it was impossible under those conditions and we both knew it.

Miss Milsted, a Lt. Colonel and a shrew, was frantically infatuated with him. Everyone knew it, and he was exasperated and embarrassed by her obvious intentions. He avoided her as much as he could. At one point he decided to have a minor hernia repaired, knowing that it could become more serious at some point in the future when the repair would not be so easily available. The word went around that he would be operated on at a certain time. He was wheeled into the operating room, having been anesthetized with a spinal injection previously, rendering him completely numb below the waist. He was placed on the operating table and a screen placed below his chin so he could not see the operating "field." I was "scrubbing" that day, so was waiting, gowned and gloved, my instrument table arranged precisely, to assist the surgeon who had not yet made an appearance. The covering sheet was removed in preparation for prepping the groin area, at which point Miss Milsted sailed into the room, announcing that she could not trust the medics to perform the prep properly and would assume the task herself. But I was startled and excited by the sight of his beautiful uncircumcised cock that hung low and soft to the table. I suspect that more than one person in that room was salivating over this gorgeous organ, and especially guilty over our reactions since the patient, Dr. Corey and a personal acquaintance, could not see or be aware of what was happening.

Miss Milsted picked up the sponge stick, gripped a gauze sponge with it, dipped it in the soap mixture, and began to "scrub" the groin area in the prescribed fashion. She started in the middle of the area and gradually moved outward in concentric circles until the entire area had been scrubbed once. As she proceeded in her task, we all became aware that Dr. Corey's cock was enlarging. Gradually the darker head began to emerge from the foreskin, the organ elongating slowly. Miss Milsted quickly replaced the sponge with a clean one and repeated her ministrations. The room was totally silent, as if we were all holding our breaths. More and more the beautiful cock responded, becoming longer and longer, gathering tumescence. Miss Milsted seemed to be breathing a little deeper as she continued, repeating the tantalizing process over and over. The rule was to scrub for five minutes; five, six minutes passed, and she showed no signs of being satisfied with her work. I don't know what Dr. Corey, conscious but sedated, thought was happening during that period, except that he was waiting for the surgery to begin.

Finally the process was complete, meaning that the cock was entirely rigid and standing bolt upright like an alert sentinel ready for action. The same could be said for me and probably many of the others, especially Miss Milsted. Since I was wearing a gown over my pajamas in preparation for assisting, my reaction, thankfully, was concealed. I did not dare to look at Claude who was circulating that day, clad in the usual loose pajamas, since any major reaction would be more difficult for him to conceal.

After about ten minutes had passed, with constant manipulation of the magnificent equipment, and seeing that there was no more length or tumescence to develop, she appeared satisfied with her work. Dr. Corey had the cleanest groin that had ever existed, that was clear. Finally she allowed the rest of us to proceed, to drape the patient and summon the surgeon who would, finally, be able to do the surgery. As soon as she stopped her ministrations, the tumescence was lost and it returned to its usual state (which was in itself impressive). It was rumored that the head nurse pursued the poor man even more persistently after that, but I am pretty sure she never got what she wanted from Dr. Corey.

Dr. Robert Mills was my favorite of all the doctors who trained us. He was head of the training program, provided many of the lectures on various aspects of medicine and surgery, and had his own office near the ward. He was a stocky, dark-eyed, dark-haired Texan, soft-spoken but tireless, and more medically oriented than some of his colleagues; he was almost as knowledgeable about the psychology and physiology of his patients as about the surgical aspects, which was somewhat unusual. He had a receding hairline which I found to be decidedly sexy.

While I enjoyed the surgery I was not happy in my duties on the ward, caring for surgical patients, because the head nurse, a friend of Miss Milsted's, was a harridan. When Dr. Mills perceived my discomfort, he began to call me into his office in the late afternoons, in part to anger the nurse and also to disarm the situation. This became a regular event, one that I looked forward to.

The first time I was summoned to his office, I expected to be scolded for something. Instead, when I came in the office, Dr. Mills said for me to fetch the chart of a particular patient. When I returned with the chart, he began to talk about the patient's medical problems and then asked me to retrieve a book from his book shelf and read passages from a certain section of the book. He leaned back in his leather chair, deep in thought, although he probably knew more about the subject than the author of the book. We then discussed the problem, which I remember involved a probable adrenal insufficiency, which could complicate his surgical situation. Some of what he said went over my head, but he was careful to explain the physiology in basic enough terms so I understood the general concepts involved.

At first I was confused by the special attention I was receiving, but later I became convinced that it helped him in considering the patient to verbalize and receive responses from me. At least I was able to ask intelligent questions. A few times I caught him omitting a detail, and when I interjected that detail he praised me for remembering. It was an obvious teaching ploy, but one I appreciated. His eyes would sparkle and hold my gaze as long as I gazed back. I adored him.

One day he asked if I were a California surfer. I replied shortly that I had never been on a surf board. I was getting a little tired of that question. He didn't ask any personal questions again, but I knew it was an implied compliment, that I had a fit, swimmer's body and he appreciated it. Nothing more.

The nurse was incensed that he would take away one of her staff and one of her charts on his own whim, and after a few minutes of our session she would begin to knock on the door, demanding the patient's chart back. Implicit was her disapproval of the time he spent with me.

Eventually he stopped asking for the chart, and told me to lock the door when I entered to avoid being disturbed by the nurse.

One day he was facing the rear wall when I entered, his feet up on the furniture, and I could tell he was thinking about one of his problem cases. After hearing the door lock click and without even turning around, he waved over his shoulder in the general direction of the book case. "Get me that thick green book on the second shelf, Bristow," he said in his Texas drawl. "Read me what it says about the bladder neck."

I read about a page of largely foreign phrases, all about the lower abdomen, rectum, and urinary bladder, and stumbled on the word "prostate," pronouncing it "prostrate." He didn't mention the error then, but we talked about various aspects of a particular patient's diagnosis and prognosis, and then he mentioned the word, "prostate," again.

"Do you know what that is, Bristow?" I wasn't sure and said so. "Didn't the doctor doing your physical in recruitment put his finger up your ass?" I shook my head, thinking that it was probably a good thing because that might have disturbed the precarious situation even more at that time. "Shit," he said mildly. "They don't even do a decent entry physical. Come here, Bristow."

I went to stand in front of him. "Turn around and drop your pants," he said in a conversational tone. I did as he ordered, leaving my shorts in place but hitching up my shirt. A moment of silence followed but then I felt his touch on both sides as he stripped down my shorts, leaving my bare ass in his face. I blushed but did not move away. His hands returned to my waist, resting gently on my hips. I began to quiver, his touch suddenly significant, enticing.

"The prostate gland is found about a finger's length up

80

the rectum, although when you feel the prostate you are palpating it through the rectal wall since it really surrounds the urethra, just below the bladder neck, anteriorly." I tried to pay attention to his words but his touch was magic.

"I'm going to put some lubricant on my finger and palpate your prostate. In addition to completing your physical exam, you will be able to experience the sensation and know what other men are feeling when you do the palpation yourself." Was it my imagination or was his voice also a little shaky, a little tense? His words were detached, scientific. I couldn't see his face which I thought might be quite revealing.

From his desk drawer he extracted a small tube of lubricant and smeared some on his finger. "Bend over, Bristow," he breathed, and I knew his voice was different. I could feel his finger gently probing, first in little circles around my opening and then directly inside. My legs began to shake noticeably. It had been some time since Craig had initiated me, and I was not experienced by any means.

"Lean your elbows on the desk there and bend your knees. Just relax and let me in," he ordered softly. I did as I was told, and felt his finger enter, gradually move deeper, and soon touch a sensitive spot. It wasn't painful at all, in fact it stirred my most lascivious fantasies. He began to move his finger, and I groaned with pleasure.

"I'm massaging the top of the walnut-shaped gland now," he said, moving his finger from side to side. "The upper poles of the organ are the most sensitive. If there were a cancer there, it would probably be palpable. In your case the shape is entirely normal, as I would expect it to be at your age. . . In fact it's — very nice." My knees quivered and involuntarily I pushed back against his probing, his magic finger deep inside. I thought I knew what he meant by "nice." I could feel my cock becoming hard, and wanted

81

more of whatever he was able to give me. I was not embarrassed by my erection. I knew he was my friend.

"Yes, it feels good, doesn't it," he breathed. "I can feel it pulsating in there, swelling a little. That's what happens when sexual excitement is occurring. Remember that." Another greased finger entered me, and I wanted more. My sphincter was relaxing.

"Please, sir − Major," the words were wrenched from my soul, "Please. . . "

"Yes, I understand," he said, his voice thick and almost as emotionally-laden as mine.

His fingers were removed, leaving an aching void. I heard his zipper going down and the rustle of his pants dropping to the floor, and then a pause. A moment later I felt him enter me, slowly, deliberately, tenderly, and I pushed back, impatient to be filled by him. Quickly I felt my prostate pressed again, this time by a burgeoning soft−hard presence that I vaguely recognized, vaguely realized was real Texas manhood. "Oh, Christ, Matt," he groaned, pressing deeply just as I wanted. "Yes," I whispered encouragingly. "Yes!" In the next few moments it became clear to me that Craig's instructions in the mountain-top cabin had not been in vain, and that I had sorely missed that kind of man−to−man contact.

He hugged me to him; I felt his crisp hairs grinding against me and his hot breath on my cheek, and it was good. My satisfaction was magnified by the obvious evidence that I was capable of bringing pleasure to Dr. Mills.

He spasmed long and hard, and when he was finished I straightened up and turned around. His face was radiant and loving, and then he looked down. "Oh, Matt, come here," he gasped, gripping my bobbing erection in his strong surgeon's fist. He knelt and engulfed me. Within seconds the dam overflowed and he moaned appreciatively when

I thrust hard against him.

Finally he rose, wiping his mouth with the back of his hand. He smiled at me, his eyes wide and approving. "Hmmm, that's good. High protein." Scientifically correct even then.

10

Wes and I became buddies, in that we went almost everywhere together and sometimes drifted off to sleep in our neighboring beds in the middle of whispered conversation. My admiration of him and his attitude of ignoring invitations to intimacy grew more difficult as time went on, however; I found myself dreaming about having sex with him, his trim body only a step away across the cubicle, but I had to curb my fantasies, I knew.

Letters from home were sparse. My father had never been one to write letters, and Craig, after one apologetic letter saying most of the things he had said during my furlough, discontinued his post office box for private mail. I received more letters from Maria than from any of the family. Before I left I had taken Daisy to her and asked her to take care of her if possible. I explained to Daisy that she could stay with Maria as long as she wanted, and Maria's instant mother instinct took over from there. Daisy was suspicious at first, as usual, but warmed to Maria's innately caring ways. I sent Maria some money at sporadic intervals for Daisy's expenses.

One of the great things about Washington D.C. was the influx of secretaries and office workers from all along the eastern seaboard in response to the war. It was Wes who tipped me off to the dances and other social events scheduled frequently in down-town Washington at various hotels and social halls arranged to fill the gap in their social lives. Wes took me there one night, and that's when I met Kathleen.

She was from North Carolina, and in many ways a typical product of those times of mobilization. She was third in a family of six children, and two older brothers had already gone to the Army. When she graduated from secretarial school, there were few opportunities in her home town, but Washington, with its massive office bureaucracies, beckoned with career possibilities. Thus she joined the huge army of single country girls handling office jobs throughout the city.

She had the most stunning red hair I had ever seen, and I loved playing with it when we became better acquainted. She seemed shy at first, but I soon learned that was largely a facade of gentility to mask an avarice for men. After our second date she managed to arrange dates for her two room mates, and we had one of the bedrooms to ourselves for a few hours. It quickly became apparent that she was as sex-starved as I, and also that she was much more experienced in making a man happy than I had assumed. Later I learned that her older brothers had taught her all she needed to know. She was surprised that I was shocked by this admission; apparently the practice of serious incestuous exploration was not unusual in her country town.

Her red pubic hair became a fetish of mine for oral sex. Perhaps I carried it too far sometimes because she was sometimes almost in tears of frustration when we finally came to penetration. I still had not developed an appreciation of condoms but she was happy to finish orally, with a technique that I could not seriously criticize. I am quite sure she dated other men, and probably slept with them sometimes, but she at least pretended that she was hurt if I expressed interest in other women.

I was curious about her experience with her brothers. "Did you ever have sex with both of them at the same time?" I asked. Again she looked shocked at such an idea. "No, no, of course not. Usually Roy (the younger one) would wait until Robert finished," she explained. "I really liked Roy better, so that was OK with me."

85

"What about your sister?"

She looked blankly at me. "What about her?"

"Did you two ever have sex?"

At first she looked shocked, but finally admitted that they had played sometimes. "There is something about that, sex with another woman, that is really exciting," she finally confessed. I thought it strange that, while she had little hesitation in confiding of her sexual activities with her brothers, admitting to lesbian contact seemed distressing. I pushed a little further.

"How about – your room mates?" It was a shot in the dark that paid off.

She turned away from me abruptly, but I put my arm around her, caressing one breast the way she liked it, and she finally murmured, "Sometimes."

It required many weeks of teasing and cajoling, but finally she arranged for me to meet one of her room mates with the possibility of arranging a three-way. Becky was from Alabama with an even more marked accent, but blond and buxom. Her hips were unusually narrow, emphasizing her voluminous breasts. When we were introduced she looked me over like a buyer of a stud horse, I thought, but apparently I passed muster. She had a somewhat mercenary streak, however; I had to take both girls to a very expensive dinner, which I could ill afford, before we managed to share the same bed.

My only other such experiences had been with Craig and Daisy, never with two women, and I soon learned that "triple-plays" can be fraught with difficulties if not handled expertly. I had entered, or really inserted myself, into a relationship that was apparently on-going between the two girls. Probably both girls viewed me as a potential threat for the attentions of their girl friend. While Becky didn't seem to resent my sleeping with Kathleen in the usual arrangement, believing that to be acceptable because it was "normal," my presence disturbed the routine that the two girls apparently followed when they were together. While I enjoyed watching them make love to each other, I was always frustrated if I was not taking an active role in one way or another. Clearly for me another man in the scene was more satisfying.

The next night, after lights out in the dorm, I related the evening's events to Wes, whispering across the narrow chasm between our beds. Winter had come to Washington and a storm had started that morning. By evening freezing rain was slanting against the windows, but it was almost too warm inside.

"A real three-way? Oh, yeah?" he whispered dubiously. "Tell me about it."

"Well, they went in the bedroom first, forbidding me to join them for ten minutes. Anyway, I got undressed in the living room and finally walked in, already erect just thinking about what was going to happen. There was a little bedside lamp with a pink shade — don't you hate those stupid little frilly things? They barely give enough light to even tie your shoes."

"Who gives a shit about the lamp?" he growled. "What happened then?"

I smiled in the dark. I began to wonder if he was playing with himself. I had never seen any evidence of his masturbating in the months we had shared the cubicle, and we rarely spoke much about sex. That thought started me on that track, and I gripped myself under the blanket.

"Well, they were lying on the bed, of course, looking at me and giggling. Of course both sets of eyes went directly to my crotch, but that didn't bother me. I guess I do all right in that department."

There was a faint sound from the other bed. Had he

87

murmured, "I'll say"? I decided to pretend I hadn't heard.

"Anyway, I crawled into bed between them, and right away there was this hesitation, like there was a wall between us, it seemed. I didn't know what to do first, and they didn't really seem to be interested in doing anything with me!"

I was sure that I could detect his hand moving under his blanket. I almost forgot what I was saying.

"You've met Kathleen, of course, so you know she's got pretty nice breasts but nothing to write home about. Well, Becky is something else! I focused on those pretty things and she started to warm up, and then I reached out for Kathleen and sort of brought her into the picture, and eventually they started on me a little. At first we were all oral, you know, but Becky's not nearly as expert as Kathleen, and I don't think she likes it all that much."

I stopped for a minute, remembering how it felt, the differences between the two partners, the constant availability of their willing bodies that made three-ways so fascinating.

"Go on!" Wes croaked, and there was no denying his involvement now in the story, and in his flailing hand.

"Well," I grinned to myself, "eventually I just moved back and forth between them, penetrating first one and then the other, and I think they both had a couple of orgasms. It's hard to tell with women, you know? But pretty soon I couldn't hold back any longer. Kathleen started with her mouth and then Becky came over to help, and that's how it ended, more or less. They got each other off again while I watched. I thought I should get back to the base before the storm arrived, but they didn't even get dressed when I got up to put my clothes on. They just lay there, sprawled out on the bed, watching me. I suspect they went right back to it with each other after I left."

"Ugh!" he groaned, and I knew what was happening. I followed quickly, but I knew that it was his excitement that brought my climax. I wanted badly to be there in bed with him, my face in his crotch, when the explosion occurred.

Kathleen, Becky, and I had a couple more three-ways, but it was never totally satisfying for me, mostly because of Becky's restraint or possibly resentment. She was quite possessive of Kathleen when I was there.

The last time we were together we got into an argument. I guess Becky thought I was being too aggressive and made some disparaging remarks about "men and their penises." I didn't really understand her problem with penises, since she seemed to get along fine with mine, although not devoted to it, by any means.

"You men act like you can swagger around and get anything you want, just because of what's swinging between your legs." (She was sometimes pretty vulgar.)

I thought about it for a minute, decided that the situation had deteriorated beyond hope, and then summarized the way I felt about men. "Well, yes, I guess our penises are pretty important to us. A man just steps out into traffic with a certain confidence, a certain aggressiveness and masculinity, that is sort of based on his potential, and I suppose his penis is, in a way, at least a symbol of his base of operations."

"So where does that leave us women?" she demanded gruffly. Again I had to stop and think of just how I felt.

"Women don't have penises and shouldn't act like they do," I stated finally. "That's not what women are about. They are our partners, our nurturers, our more sensitive counterparts, without which men would just be warriors or farmers or roamers."

Becky wasn't happy with that, either. She crouched on

the other side of Kathleen and glared at me. "That makes women inferior to men, then."

"Not as far as I'm concerned. But the more sensitive and loving she is, the more attractive she is to me. Feminine men aren't attractive to me any more than masculine women. Both men and women need to be confident in their gender roles that compliment each other – different but not unequal. I guess the way a woman moves, swinging her hips in that typically feminine, 'come hither' way and sometimes wearing clothes that encourage peeks at the tops of her breasts, at least, is the counterpart of a man's what-you-call 'swagger'."

Kathleen listened to us but did not take part in the discussion. I think she agreed with me but did not want to antagonize Becky. I wondered how they got along when I wasn't there.

Wes and I had developed a routine of playing tennis in the evenings after the meal when we were both free. He had taught me the game, but soon I was winning at least half the time. With the winter discouraging outdoor activities, we spent more time in the dorm and frequently the subject of conversation revolved around telepathy.

Several times we had had the experience of feeling that we knew what the other was thinking about before he verbalized his thought, and so we began to "exercise" our telepathic potential. We would lie quietly on our beds, trying to clear our minds for a few minutes, ignoring the ordinary dorm sounds around us. One of us would be designated the "sender" and the other the "receiver," and the receiver would try to describe what scene or situation the sender was initiating. It was fun, and we were sometimes startled at how close we could come to correct interpretation of the other's thoughts. It was a reflection of the closeness of our relationship, but we didn't discuss that. The only problem was the frequent, unwelcome noises that intruded, since we were in a group setting with eighteen other men, all coming and going, laughing or swearing, banging locker doors, and so forth, which disturbed our concentration.

I received a promotion in April, probably directly because of Dr. Mills' recommendation, and Wes and I decided to celebrate. I had an idea.

"I'll spring for a quiet hotel room for both of us, with all this increase in pay I'm getting (I think it amounted to eighteen dollars), and we can try out our telepathy without all this noise. How about that?"

Wes looked at me with interest. "Yeah, that ought to be interesting. I'm sure if we didn't have all this noise around that we could really communicate on a sub-conscious level. Let's do it!"

The following week we checked into an old hotel downtown, the Willard, and made our preparations. There was one double bed in the room so we could lie closely enough together to "communicate" without disturbance. We both showered, remaining very quiet, not talking except when necessary; we turned out the light and lay on the bed, one facing one way and the other facing the other way. This was supposed to improve our transmission as compared to the usual side-by-side position. I concentrated on the dimly–visible tawdry picture on the wall that I faced, and he had another picture on the opposite wall to concentrate on. He took first turn as "sender," and I more or less correctly interpreted his "transmission" as a scene beside a creek in the woods. In my turn I "sent" an image of a tall, crumbling barn, but he could only interpret the image as a wooden building, not the entire concept.

When trying to clear our minds, we had discovered that thoughts tended to wander until supposedly focused by the image being transmitted. Being this close to Wes, my mind began to wander to sex. If I looked at him I could see almost every muscle in his chest and arms and legs, etched clearly in the shadows, only inches away. I tried to blank it out, but was only partially successful. I missed some of his next transmission, mistaking a horse for a cow. When it was my turn, I concentrated on having sex with Wes, expecting that to be completely garbled in transmission.

He did not respond for some minutes, but then he turned to me, fished through the fly of my shorts, and took me into his mouth. Of course I did the same with him. No words were exchanged, but I had never been "plugged into" another person as intimately as I was to Wes at that moment. I could feel every muscle when I pulled him to me. His buttocks were flexing melons in my hands. Our sex was dreamlike, slow and deliberate, thoroughly exploratory, and when our climaxes came they occurred simultaneously as gentle flows with long, tapering peaks. Even then we did not release each other before falling asleep, the other's taste fresh in our mouths.

In the morning I awoke rearranged in bed in the usual orientation, my morning hardon extending through the fly of my regulation shorts, and with Wes' eyes, only about a foot away with his head on his pillow, studying my face. Frequently, attractive people are not so attractive when you get so close that all the minor blemishes show up. It wasn't that way with Wes; he was really a flawlessly handsome man. His eyes crinkled a little smile as I opened my eyes.

"You planted that idea in my brain, didn't you?"

"Uh huh," I grinned back, stretching luxuriously and feeling no guilt whatsoever.

"Maybe the thought had been there all along," he suggested.

"Uh huh."

"Matt, I — I want to be your friend, even your best friend, but — I don't think we should be lovers. Not as things are."

I was crestfallen but immediately understood. "Yeah, I guess you're right," I sighed. "I suppose it's better that way, too many uncertainties. . . but as my best friend do you think you should be gripping my hardon that way?"

He chuckled, his grip becoming even more possessive. "Come here, Napa-noodle." This time our sex was rough and tumble, almost greedy, perhaps because we knew it would be the last time. My fantasies had come true briefly, at least. That would have to satisfy me for the time being. I was learning that not every guy was fair game.

Although my training class had concluded and most of the others in my class had been scattered to other assignments, I did not receive orders out but remained at the base. I continued to work in the operating room from time to time with Dr. Mills, sometimes teaching the newer students, but was relieved of the ward duties due to his intervention. I soon learned the real reasons.

"You know," Dr. Mills started one day in his office, "we at Walter Reed are expected to set the standards for the entire Army Medical Corps. You also know that America has not been involved in a real ground war for about twenty-five years, and it is an enormous task to get things organized."

He was tilted back in his chair, smoking his pipe which he only did when deep in thought, I had learned. The fact that he was involving me in these considerations did not surprise me, because he had shared many of his responsibilities with me from time to time over the last several months.

"I've been relieved of the surgery training job, as of tomorrow. My real task now is to design modules for aid stations close to battle zones, develop supply lists, logistics, and instruction manuals for handling casualties under all possible conditions. I know you haven't had any experience in the field but you're bright, you have a logical mind, you handle yourself well at the operating table, and I know I can count on you for help and feedback. Because you're not so experienced, you can detect wording that might confuse the readers. I'd like to keep you here on that assignment. That is, if you want to. It's strictly a volunteer situation."

I think he knew that I would have done anything he asked me, including shoulder a rifle, but he wasn't taking me for granted.

"You should continue your exposure to surgery, because you can't learn enough, ever, about the human body and the ways it can go wrong. Eventually you'll see situations in the field that will challenge your most extreme concepts. I will still do some selected surgery and I want you to assist me with that. In particular I want to teach you more about suturing, because you'll probably be doing a lot of that. But when you're not tied up in the operating room, I want you to help me with this special project. OK?"

"Yes, sir," I said with my greatest sincerity.

He peered at my face and chuckled at my grave expression. "It's not going to be all slogging, grinding drudgery, you know. But there will be long hours sometimes and a lot of leg work."

Our relationship had ripened in the months we had been working together. I had met his wife, Reba, a demure "Georgia peach" as he called her. From seeing them together and overhearing telephone calls I knew that their home and sex life was rich and full, but occasionally, sometimes at several week intervals, he and I had our own kind of sex, usually at times when there were special problems in his work. Sex seemed to be therapeutic for him, but he was never casual or impersonal with me. Although I might be bent over a desk or bracing myself against a wall, I felt his love and tenderness and need for me as a person as clearly as his thick presence in my body, and I was happy with that.

When we worked together in the operating room he would frequently teach me, and other men in later training classes, the differences between surgery under sterile conditions and controlled environments and what we would encounter in the field. Piercing wounds were not all that different from incisional ones, he pointed out. There were the same layers of the body to repair, using similar techniques, and if we didn't know the "normal" we could not be expected to understand the abnormal. Blast wounds, where large areas were blown away, were a larger challenge, but could be approached in similar ways. He could make the subject not only palatable, in a grizzly sort of way, but also fascinating to all of us.

I was also happy, for the most part, with my relationship with Kathleen. When away from Becky she was a joy. I almost enjoyed shopping for groceries and other ordinary errands with her, and our infrequent disagreements were short and never outlasted the day. Although her jealousy was sometimes annoying, we had become playful in our sexual romps. She gradually lost what few inhibitions she had had, even accepting anal sex on occasion, and I looked forward to our weekly dates. I was aware, however, of missing the masculine element which was an important part of my sexuality and which she could not provide. Perhaps we were so compatible because she was taught sex by her randy brothers and understood men's natural aggressiveness, but she had learned how to get and take what she wanted, also.

There was a constant turnover of personnel on the base. It seemed the entire country was on the move brought on by the war. Some of the draftees were well beyond their youth, and it made for a heterogeneous Army. Of the twenty inhabitants of my dorm, Wes and I were the only men left from the complement there when I arrived. Sometimes there were temptations to become close to one of the new men, but they were usually shipped out a few weeks or months later to be replaced by another one of a different stripe.

A few of them were rather obviously available. One husky medic from West Virginia made it a habit to strut around the dorm in the evenings with a rather massive erection distorting the towel draped around his middle, practically asking for service, but I stayed clear. For a few weeks a cute guy from Los Angeles, his hair a mass of tight, golden curls, occupied the bed across the dorm from me; several times, late at night, we jacked off, each in his own bed, while watching the other. It was fun and satisfying in some ways. Then he left for duty in Africa, and I never saw him again.

Wes seemed even more preoccupied with his duties than usual as time passed and our military efforts through the world became more extensive. British troops weren't doing too well in Africa. At the Casablanca conference, the American General Eisenhower had been named Supreme Commander. In July our troops invaded Sicily en route to Italy and began to bomb Rome. Wes always seemed to be unusually busy or away on TDY (temporary duty) when some big event was occurring. When he was "home" our attempts at telepathic communication seemed to become less effective, perhaps because we had more difficulty in clearing our minds of the day-to-day issues. I also found myself thinking back to that night with him in the hotel, and those thoughts interfered with my concentration.

The day I turned twenty-one he suggested going to a downtown bar that he was familiar with by way of celebration. We took the bus to the general neighborhood and walked the rest of the way along dark, almost empty streets. Street lights were dimmed to save energy. Still a "hick" from a small California town, I was always awed by the power residing in this capitol city, in the monumental buildings that housed the headquarters of the mysterious seats of government, and the enormous numbers of people working night and day as part of the war-mobilization program. That night, as usual, at least half the pedestrians on the eerily-quiet streets were in uniform. Dark, closed cars with government license plates cruised by, probably on their way to important meetings, we assumed; they were the only vehicles whose owners didn't suffer from gas rationing.

Only a few blocks from the White House, the bar was a large room resembling an old-fashioned library with walls lined with books on shelves; it was dimly lit, filled with small tables for four, and there was a piano player who seemed to know everybody. He played requests from people he liked and ignored those from people he didn't take a fancy to. His version of "You'd Be So Nice To Come Home To" sent delicious shivers up my spine.

The social structure of bars in Washington was different from that in California. It was illegal to stand at a bar or to carry your drink with you. Everyone was required to sit at a table with his or her drink, although it was permitted to visit other tables without carrying a drink. It seemed as if it would be awkward to become acquainted with other people in the bar under these rules, but no one else seemed to mind. Wes frequently glanced around the bar as if looking for a familiar face. Many of the tables were occupied by two men. Finally we made eye contact with two attractive women at another table and eventually asked the waiter to move us in order to join them, but they turned out to be boring conversationalists and we went home alone.

It was our second time in the bar when a single man entered and scanned the room as if looking for someone in particular. Wes also noticed him; after a moment the stranger came to our table and asked politely if he could join us. This was not unusual because, if all the tables were even partially occupied, new arrivals were required to share tables in order to have a drink. He seemed friendly, fortyish with a little paunch that his well-tailored, dark suit concealed quite well, and introduced himself as Harley. Wes seemed a little tense, but eventually joined our casual conversation. Harley appeared to be very friendly with the piano player, and was obviously a frequent customer in the bar. He went to talk to the pianist once, but I noticed the player shook his head with a smile.

"So where are you guys from?" It was the standard question since practically everyone was from somewhere else, the frenetic wartime strangeness. I replied California (I knew by now that no one had ever heard of Napa) and Wes mentioned Panama. Harley was not surprised.

"I'm from Manhattan, myself," he said pointedly, and his eyes swiveled to Wes. Wes stared at the wall for a minute, but made no comment. "I've never been to New York," I responded.

We were all drinking Tom Collins cocktails, and by midnight, which was bar closing time, I felt rather high. Harley casually mentioned that he was going to a party that night, and invited us along. I was always ready for a party. Wes looked at him a little sharply but offered no objection, so we piled into a taxi that miraculously waited at the curb. We followed the streetcar with its overhead wire contact for a while up Wisconsin Avenue and then turned off, ending up in the Northwest section of the city made up mostly of large, brick apartment buildings.

The lobby of the building was rather luxuriously appointed. As we ascended in the elevator, Wes ventured, "This is a State Department building, isn't it?"

Harley replied, his voice even and almost expressionless, "It doesn't belong to the government, but many people in the building work for the State Department, yes." I didn't understand the exchange, but I was not particularly interested. I was a little giddy from the alcohol.

Harley had a key to the door, and we entered a large apartment with plush carpeting and soft lighting. There were only three people visible, young men well-dressed in civilian suits, talking quietly near a gleaming bar in the corner. They nodded to us and returned to their conversation.

"Make yourself at home," Harley invited. "I'll find our host." He knocked on a door and it was almost immediately opened by a tall, distinguished man in a tuxedo. He studied us for a moment, concentrating on Wes, it seemed, who returned his inspection. Wes turned to me.

"Why don't you help yourself at the bar, Matt? I'll get back to you later."

His dismissal seemed almost rude to me, which was very unusual for Wes. However, I moved to the bar and then looked back. Wes and Harley were joining our host in the other room, and the door was firmly closed behind them.

Since there was no bartender, I started searching around for something familiar. I finally extracted a can of beer from a tub of ice water and opened it with the tool I found on the bar. When I turned around, the men who had been clustered nearby were disappearing into another room down the hall with an open door.

I sagged into a luxurious easy chair under a dim floor lamp, sipping the tangy brew. I had almost forgotten what it was like to have comfortable surroundings, dim lights, and soft music in the background to relax in. "My Devotion," its soft phrases swelling around me, seemed an unattainable goal but a nice thought. The atmosphere was almost soporific, especially in my semi-inebriated state, but I was uncomfortable because I was alone. Where had Wes gone? What was going on down the hall? Was I actually missing the party? When no one appeared for several more minutes, I wandered down the hall to the open door.

There were certainly people in there as judged by human

100

noises and labored breathing, but it was a black hole − I could see absolutely nothing. I stood in the doorway, listening, and I remembered one previous similar experience − the bedroom in the party house in Guerneville when I was looking for Craig. I quickly excluded him from my mind, as had become my habit. I also realized vaguely that, although I could see nothing in the room, anyone looking toward the door could see me clearly in the hall light behind me.

My sense of smell told me something about what to expect. When you stand at the threshold of a woman's boudoir, you encounter the typical fragrance of perfume and cosmetics and a trace of vagina, and the latter is undefinable, unique to itself. There is sweetness there, and perhaps innocence. I react to that combination with a stirring between my legs that is relatively subtle but anticipatory. When entering a man's room, the fragrances are very different − some perspiration, perhaps some after-shave, a trace of shoe polish, and, when there is action afoot, the aphrodisiacal fragrance of semen. My reaction to that is instant rigidity. That does not mean that men are more exciting than women, but that instant desire, instant gratification is normal for men, and that includes me. This room was definitely man's country.

I started to move forward, my hand extended so I did not collide with anyone; almost immediately the hand was grasped firmly and I was pulled into the darkness. The beer was extracted from my other hand and several pairs of hands began to undress me simultaneously, one from behind and at least one on each side. It was only a few moments before I was totally stripped, and then even more groping hands made contact, caressing my chest and tweaking my nipples, stroking my bare butt, cupping my balls, massaging my stiffened cock.

My memories of the next hour or so are fragmentary.

101

I know that that short time was probably the most enjoyable period I had ever spent to that time of my life, with every conceivable libidinous desire for men indulged in repeatedly in a tangled mass of muscular bodies, shaven faces, hairy legs, accomodating butts, and aroused genitalia. It was totally anonymous. I knew no one and could have recognized no one in that stygian paradise. The thought occurred to me that one major factor that differentiates man-to-man sex from man-woman sex (for me at least) is the pleasure I take in both assertive and receptive roles; there is ecstacy in both sending and receiving, and pride in being able to take it as well as give it. That dichotomy never seems to apply as forthrightly with women.

Finally I felt my climax coming from a long way off, it seemed, and prolonged more than it seemed possible to extend it, and then the mouth bearing my sperm settled on mine to exchange a deep kiss. That was a startlingly sensuous moment, but no more startling than the man's words that followed: "I've wanted to do that for a long time, Matt." I recognized the mellifluous, heavily-accented voice of the strangely–cajun Claude Marcel.

12

A few minutes later I groped my way through the darkness to the lighted door, Claude Marcel's hand in mine. By that time I was exhausted and needed to get away from the incessant call of male sex wildness, something I wouldn't have believed possible an hour ago when all my hormones had been on full.

He had a beautifully trim ass, I noticed, and I patted and stroked it appreciatively, wondering if that had been the one that I had adored with tongue and lips earlier. Probably neither of us could be sure. I flashed back to a day at the lake at home, when I had wondered why women were interested in men's asses; I now knew why I was interested, but I doubted the same reasons applied to women. I towed him, nude and stumbling, to the living room and pulled him to the floor where we could sit and catch our breaths. Across from us was the door behind which Wes had disappeared; it was still closed.

"What was all that?" I questioned him a little breathlessly, noting his latest hair-do that seemed an attempt at unlikely glamour though the hair was not really long enough. The phonograph had switched to "Serenade in Blue."

Claude chuckled, stroking my leg, his hand gradually moving closer to my depleted crotch. "These parties go on almost every weekend. The host is a big-wig in the State Department, I think. Most of State is queer, you know, and once you get in the group, it's free sailing from there on. Some say that Under Secretary Sumner Wells is one of us. Now that you have been here once you can come again, but we keep it very hush-hush, you know. 'Loose lips sink ships,' and all that sort of thing." I hadn't encountered any loose lips that evening; they were all pretty muscular where it counted. He began to fondle my drooping equipment, apparently hoping for some renewed interest there. His own slender cock was still prominent and I held it casually, knowing it could be mine when and if I wanted it.

"So where were you sent after the class finished? I never heard."

"At first I had standby orders to the Pacific, but then an announcement went out for auditions for an Army show, and I made it! Irving Berlin's 'This Is The Army' in New York — doing more or less what I used to do in New Orleans, only in uniform, more or less. They will probably also make it into a movie."

"Huh?" I did not understand what he was talking about. Several other men emerged from the room, getting dressed, mostly in Army or Navy uniforms, and some of them officers. Obviously there was no "rank has its privileges" operating here. I didn't recognize any of them.

He grinned, seeing my confusion. "I thought maybe you'd know all about that, being from near San Francisco. I used to do drag shows on Bourbon Street, until I got drafted. The recruitment office knew my background, but they didn't seem to care. And now I'm doing it for the Army!"

"You mean — you dress in women's clothes?"

"Sure, and dance and flirt with other guys. We're so gay!"

"Gay?" That word wasn't used much in my experience.

Claude swept his hair up and struck a feminine pose, his nose tilted skyward. "That's the new term for queer, fairy, fruit! And all the 'straights' just think we mean happy!"

104

It all sounded weird to me, and something that did not include me. For the first time I felt different from other men, at least those men who enjoyed being thought of as feminine. It struck me again that I liked men because they were men, and women because they were women, but I had no interest in pretending to be something I wasn't.

There wasn't much time to reflect on the thought, since at that moment the door across the room opened and Wes emerged with Harley and the host. They were carefully attired as usual, it seemed, so it didn't look like they had had a sex scene at all. In a perverse sense I was happy about that; in the back of my mind was a small hope that I could get Wes into the dark room down the hall. . . Wes' eyes lit on Claude.

"Hey, how's it going, Claude?" he asked with a friendly smile.

"OK, just getting things straight with your roomy here," Claude answered, waving my semi-hardon in the air.

Wes grinned back, noticing my embarrassment. "Yeah, he needs a lot of that," he retorted, and turned back to the host, speaking softly. "You said von Osterhaus, and spelled –h-a-u-s?" The man in the tuxedo nodded and pulled him away with a cautious look.

"I didn't know you knew Wes," I mentioned to Claude. I did not remember any contact between them during the surgery course.

"Actually I ran into him in New York while we were in rehearsals."

"New York?" I echoed. Wes hadn't said anything about being in New York, but he never volunteered anything about his short duty trips.

"Yes, some project he was involved with." "Project?" "I guess so. He said 'Manhattan Project,' but then we were in Manhattan, so I thought that was a little redundant."

"Did you, uh— sleep together?" I asked, not wanting to admit how I felt about it.

"Well, he needed a place to stay and I had a hotel room all to myself, and I was just being neighborly. . ." he wore a devilish glint. "Is that a problem?"

Wes walked over to us. "Ready to go, Matt?"

I scrambled up and Claude reluctantly released me. "Sure, I guess — if I can find my clothes." They were piled in a not–very–neat pile in one corner of the room that was now unoccupied but dimly illuminated with a small shaded lamp on a polished desk. I could see that Claude would have liked some more one-on-one with me, but Wes seemed to be acting a little strange, grim, almost, and I thought I should leave with him.

"Guess I'll head toward Ninth Street," Claude heaved an exaggerated sigh, "if you have to rush off."

"There is a car waiting to take us back to the base," Wes announced as I appeared more or less in uniform. "Huh?" my eyes bulged in surprise. "Courtesy of our host," Wes added, with a nod toward the door that was again closed. I decided I had a lot to learn about how things were done in Washington, or at least in the State Department.

As we rode to the base in the long black limousine through the dimmed–out streets, I brought up the New York angle. "Claude says he met you in New York." "Uh huh." "And you had sex?" As soon as I said it I realized how that sounded, like a jealous wife or something. Feminine. The very thing I had mentally criticized in Claude.

Wes sighed and looked sternly at me. "We discussed that, you know — no entanglements between you and me, right?"

I should have dropped the subject, but I didn't. "Is he part of your 'Manhattan project'?"

106

Wes swung sharply toward me. "Where did you hear about that?"

"Claude mentioned that you were in Manhattan for a project."

Wes gripped me hard in the shoulder, painfully so, until I cringed under his pressure. "Just forget you ever heard about the Manhattan Project, understand, Matt? You never heard about any such thing." He looked suspiciously at the driver in the front seat who seemed entirely involved in his driving through the dark, empty streets of the city. "I suppose he has clearance," he muttered.

"Also, what's happening on Ninth Street?" I thought it best to change the subject.

"Mostly bars for queers. The MPs raid it all the time. Best to stay far away from Ninth Street."

"I wish the Army would make up its mind about us," I sighed. "One day they act like having sex with another guy is some major criminal offense, and the next day it is a simple mental thing and not much of a problem."

Wes nodded. "Even the President can't seem to make up his mind. Sumner Wells is one of his best friends, they say, and there are lots of rumors about him." I wasn't sure who this Wells guy was. "There are also rumors about Eleanor."

The limousine was nearing the gates to Walter Reed. Wes tapped the driver's shoulder. "Better stop here," he said. "I don't think you want to be seen getting out of this car," he muttered to me. "And I've got an errand to do before I call it a night."

More mystery. I stared at the big, black car with the peculiar license plates as it sped away into the night and wondered if I would ever learn the whole story about my best friend. It was clear he wasn't headed for Ninth Street.

13

Kathleen and I had settled down to a semi-married status, although it took some arranging to have the apartment to ourselves. That Christmas, her two roommates went home for the holidays so we put up a Christmas tree and had a quiet holiday together. While it was comforting to pretend to be a settled heterosexual couple, especially at Christmas, I could see that boredom could be a major problem for me if this were to be the exclusive routine for the rest of my life as the wedding vows insisted. Sexually we were very compatible, but I missed the almost automatic understanding of other men to social and political thoughts and conversation. On the other hand, I missed the sensitivity and the thoughtful dependency of women when spending all my time with men, even when I was sexually in tune with them.

More and more I was becoming uneasy because my life was so safe, so removed from the battles raging all around the world. Sometimes we operated on Army casualties flown back from Europe, mostly, with complicated wounds that had received only preliminary attention overseas. I could tell that Dr. Mills was also losing patience with the project he had been assigned because it was taking so long.

He was now a Lt. Colonel, a promotion he richly deserved, but he didn't seem very impressed with such things. Of course I congratulated him but his arms were around his wife at the promotion party, and I just got a glass of champagne. At the office he sounded more and more aggravated over the phone with suppliers and some of the Army higher brass, complaining that the war was being fought with inadequate equipment and organization while he (and I) was fighting the bureaucracy in Washington. Sometimes I wanted to take him in my arms, soothe his anxieties, and give him the kind of sex he needed to cool his fever – but I suppose his wife was doing that in her way. When he and I had sex, he was masterful, certainly not gentle but always in charge, and I loved it that way. His need for me was different but there were overlaps.

That spring I received an unexpected letter from my father stating that he was getting remarried and wondered if I could get a furlough for the ceremony in early June. He even offered to send me money for the fare across country. I hadn't taken furlough since coming to Walter Reed, and Dr. Mills approved the request, although a little nervously. We never knew what the next week or month might bring, since orders to join the next anticipated invasion force in Europe were thought likely; of course no one knew when or where that might occur. The war in Italy was proceeding rather slowly after the landing at Anzio, and our forces had landed on Kwajalein in the Pacific with terrible casualties on both sides. Soon I was on a transcontinental flight to San Francisco with four engines roaring just outside the windows, relieved to be away from the tension and trying to put myself in a festive mood for my father's happy occasion.

We had arranged to meet at the Armed Forces lounge on the second floor of the main building at the airport, but I arrived a little early. There were dozens of men in uniform from all services, some asleep, sprawled in chairs while waiting for an outgoing flight. Many wore rows of combat ribbons for action in the Pacific theater, mostly: Guadalcanal, Bougainville, Tarawa. I was embarrassed by my undecorated chest.

Leaving my luggage with the attendant in the lounge, I headed for the men's room and found it also bustling with guys in uniform, not all involved with strictly excretory functions. Many of them were having sex, frankly and openly, with little concern for secrecy. Their temporary freedom, away from the battle fronts or constraints of their duty stations, made for a sort of hysterical relaxation of the "rules." Even the MPs and Shore Patrol were joining in. A Marine Private, half a leg missing, supported himself with crutches while a Quartermaster Sergeant serviced him, kneeling at his foot. I had barely finished at the urinal when a Navy Lt.j.g. had my cock down his throat and finished me off gloriously in less than a minute.

Still a little breathless, I returned to the lounge area and found my father, looking a little grayer but healthy, waiting for me. Along with him were Maria, beaming like a mother, and a strikingly beautiful, tall black-haired young woman who smiled tentatively as I approached. Dad hugged me briefly in welcome as did Maria, and then I turned to the woman, expecting an introduction to my new stepmother. Instead there was a moment of silence; I met her questioning eyes and Maria smiled, "You don't recognize her, do you?"

"Daisy?" I gasped, the solemn, cautious light in her eyes the only recognizable aspect of her appearance.

"Yes," she murmured in a low, musical voice, the first word I had ever heard from her lips. It was difficult to believe that a little makeup, a becoming dress, and high-heeled shoes could be responsible for the transformation I saw in her.

Maria giggled and took my arm possessively as we left the lounge to find the car in the parking lot. "Daisy is beginning to come out of her shell," she explained. "She still doesn't talk very much and is very shy with strangers, but sometimes we carry on long conversations while doing the housework. She has been so excited about your return. She has been reluctant to leave the house before, but she wanted to come with us today. I think she is very fond of you."

"It must be your motherly instincts that are responsible for bringing her out of that shell." I turned to Daisy, who was hanging back shyly, and took her hand. She flushed, hurrying to catch up with us, and smiled broadly at me. Her smile was worth the trip, I decided. Her grip on my hand was warm and inviting. "By the way," Maria continued, "her name is actually Helen. I don't know where the name 'Daisy' came from."

I grinned at Daisy, both of us remembering the day we met at the little cabin on the hill, and she smiled back. For the moment that was our secret. "Call me Daisy," she murmured to me, and I nodded. The name was part of her new life.

The Golden Gate bridge was bright in the warm afternoon sunshine, wisps of fog clinging to the tops of the towers, and the green of the vineland valley brought a sense of home that I had not realized I missed. The difference from the gray streets of Washington was startling.

When we arrived at home I noticed a red-white-and-blue banner hanging in the bay window with a single blue star in it; I suddenly realized the star was for me. Later I noticed a few gold stars in other homes. Not all of Napa's sons would be returning from the war.

We found my new stepmother, Martha, in the kitchen at home, a vivacious fortyish widow almost a carbon copy of my mother in appearance. Apparently she had already taken over the household, stepping into my mother's shoes effortlessly. I supposed the transition had been easier with me out of the way. My father seemed happy about the marriage, and that was the most important factor. Dad and I spent a couple of hours around the dinner table, catching up on the news of the Napa Valley, but he seemed to understand very little of my activities at the hospital. Daisy and Maria did not join us, and Martha spent most of her time in the kitchen. The living room already showed signs of change — some new furniture which was long overdue. My room remained unchanged.

"Uh — Martha and I — that is, I — thought it would be more convenient for her to sleep here this week, with all the wedding details to handle, so — you understand?" It was likely that Martha had been sleeping here for a long time, I thought, but I tried to conceal my amusement at his discomfort. It seemed he still felt guilty about sex before marriage. I wondered how he would have reacted if he had ventured into the men's room at the airport.

My biological clock was three hours ahead of California, so I was ready for sleep early. First I visited Maria's cottage behind the main house and came back with a hesitant Daisy in tow. We waved Good Night to Dad and Martha as we ascended the stairs to my bedroom, and I chuckled at their astonished faces. After the brief episode in the men's room at the airport, a night with Daisy was just what I needed, and she was apparently starved for love, judging from her unusually rich passion.

We made love and talked and made love again until my travel fatigue put me to sleep. She remembered little of her life before she wandered into Craig's neighborhood on top of the mountain, but I got the impression that she thought she might be happier that way. She was still the most satisfying, the most delightful partner I had ever had, and even better now that we could communicate verbally. I was excited by the fascinating personality that was emerging, and deeply content to fall asleep with her in my arms. I also got a perverse pleasure from the knowledge that my father and Martha were probably doing something similar just down the hall.

14

T he wedding was to be a small affair in the chapel on the fifth, and Louisa's father was to be Best Man as he had about twenty-five years previously. Their long friendship was somewhat amazing for its solid foundation, and I wondered again if there had been, at one time in their youth, a sexual relationship between the two men. As I grew older, more mature, I found I could hope for that kind of happiness for my father without feeling strange. They always hugged in an unusually hearty, unselfconscious way on happy occasions, while very few other men were that intimate.

Craig and Sueann, who was obviously pregnant again, arrived early for the ceremony, along with little Paul, now a handsome toddler. I was relieved that Craig held little pain for me after the lapse of time. He was still a handsome man, but seemingly with premature cares etched on his somber face. I received very little sense of true closeness between the couple; Sueann seemed sullen and as rebellious as ever. She frequently barked at little Paul who character- istically wandered away from time to time in normal curiosity. When I picked him up he studied my face for a moment with his probing, dark eyes and then decided he liked me. When he gave me an accepting smile a part of my heart melted. I hoped he would not be my closest point to parenting, and felt a pang for what might have been.

Some of the neighbors had been invited, and I had to endure oohs and aahs about my being in the Army, to be told how handsome I looked in my uniform, and questioned in great detail about why the Generals didn't do thus-and-so, as if I had any inside knowledge of the situation or control over decisions of strategy. Fortunately we had little time to talk because the ceremony was to begin on time.

Maria and Daisy had stayed home to prepare for the reception that would follow the ceremony. Craig said he had not seen Daisy and did not know of her improving status. I thought it strange that he seemed to have so little concern for his previous friend. We had little to say to each other, it seemed. Louisa appeared late when the ceremony was about to begin and I had no chance to talk with her at any length. She quickly disappeared as soon as the ceremony was over.

The Rev. Paul Antonetti made a dramatic appearance as part of the priest's performance, as I thought of it. My mind swung to Claude, thinking that with his theatrical talent he could have done it much better, but he could not have been handsomer than the swarthy cleric. Martha didn't seem too impressed with him, either, but perhaps it was just that she wasn't any more involved with religion than I.

Following the ceremony there was a caravan of about ten cars from the church to our farm where the reception was held. There was the usual silliness of honking of horns and the lead car towing rattling cans behind it on the way, but I suppose Dad would have missed those pranks otherwise. I was the chauffeur for the newlyweds.

Maria, dressed in a black dress and white apron almost like a proper maid, had arranged a lavish spread on the dining room table. She muttered that she couldn't make the proper pastries because of the sugar rationing. And of course there was wine, three kinds, all from grapes grown on our own vines. It wasn't long before everyone was slightly tipsy. My father and his new bride were chatting with their friends and beaming as if getting married was really a super experience, and I was happy they were enjoying themselves. I noticed that Daisy did not leave the kitchen, but that was not surprising.

Again the priest made a dramatic but late entrance, speeding into the driveway in a fancy convertible that obviously had a European pedigree. The white canvas top was folded neatly behind the rear seat. He explained that it had been a gift from a parishioner, but he flaunted it tastelessly. Of course there was a silver filigreed cross swinging obviously from the mirror, so that made it all right, I supposed. He backed it onto the lawn, headed out, although everyone else had parked in the driveway.

Antonetti made a grab for the wine as soon as he arrived, noting that he was behind the rest of us in consumption. He carried the bottle with him, filling his glass whenever needed, and worked the room like a sports promoter, I thought. As usual the women all reacted with flustered pleasure when he approached them, but the men's faces seem to freeze, as mine did, when he attempted conversation.

Late in the afternoon little Paul was nearly dozing on his feet, having missed his afternoon nap. He became irritable, and Sueann asked if she could put him to bed in my room. I took them upstairs and we put the little guy on my bed. It was hot there, the June sun broiling down on the roof, but he didn't seem to mind. Sueann seemed impatient with him, apparently anxious to return to the party downstairs, but I told myself that she was, after all, still a child herself and with another baby on the way. She didn't seem very happy.

It was my first exposure to the warm pleasure of fatherly duties. In the relative quiet of the upstairs, he fell asleep in minutes and Sueann returned to the party, but I sat at the bedside for at least ten minutes, watching him drift into peaceful sleep, enjoying the quiet and the tender feelings that are the aura of childhood nap times. I wondered if he would grow up in a world torn with war and sacrifice as

I had, and if he did, would he have the strength to make his way through a satisfying life. It seemed particularly significant that my godson was sleeping in the only room I had ever had, in the same bed in which I had napped as a child.

When I returned to the festivities, the priest was leaning against the newel post, his glass discarded somewhere and drinking directly from the bottle. Both Sueann and Craig seemed to be hanging on his every word; Craig seemed quite friendly with the priest, and Sueann was putting on her vamp act for the priest's benefit, even with her belly distended with another baby.

As I watched, Antonetti tipped up the bottle again and found it empty. He staggered over to the table serving as the bar but did not find the same brand there.

"Just goin' to get another bottle from Maria," he slurred to Craig and Sueann, and pushed through the swinging doors to the kitchen, the empty bottle in his hand. Almost immediately a horrendous scream split the air from the kitchen — unearthly, tragic. I rushed into the kitchen.

Daisy appeared to be trying to hide behind Maria, staring wide-eyed at the priest standing near the door. "No — no — please — keep him away, please!" she sobbed wildly.

I rushed to her side, trying to take her into my arms, but she fought against me, seeming to interpret any contact as threatening. "What is it?" I shouted, although I don't think she heard me. "Please, Daisy, it's me, Matt. It's OK — " The swinging door was now filled with curious party-goers, startled from their celebration.

Abruptly Daisy seized me, finally recognizing that I was her friend. "Matt — Matt — he's the one — the one who — raped me — several years ago — I remember — keep him away, please!"

"The priest?" I gasped, looking around at Antonetti.

116

Daisy nodded, sobbing hysterically into my shoulder.

The priest, eyes glazed and staring, dropped the bottle where it shattered into small fragments, scattering widely over the tile floor. He looked around wildly, encountering only questions and hostility on our faces. He correctly surmised that his charm would not extricate him from the situation this time. He leaped for the outside door and wrenched it open, bounding down the three steps to the lawn in one jump. I started after him as did several of the men from the living room who had been watching from the door.

"Paul!" A woman was shouting at him, Sueann. She ran like an ungainly turkey across the lawn after him, and Craig was not far behind her. "Paul, wait!" she shouted again. "Sueann!" Craig was even louder. "Sueann, come back!" I returned to Daisy and put my arm around her; I couldn't leave her at that moment.

The European convertible didn't start at the first attempt, and Sueann managed to wrench the door open and sprawl inside beside the priest before the engine came to life. He wrenched it into gear and spun two troughs into the lawn as he accelerated toward the road. Craig reached the car just before it swung into the highway and managed to find a grip, pulling himself into the back seat of the open car from the side. The priest headed north with one of his "parishioners" partly hanging out the back and another trying frantically to close the swinging door to avoid being thrown out. And to top it off, the telephone began ringing shrilly in the living room.

We all stared at the departing car until it disappeared in the distance, and then I tried as gently as I could to get more information from Daisy. Eventually Martha summoned the common sense to answer the phone. My father joined me in trying to soothe Daisy, still in shock from seeing her tormentor again. When we seemed to have little success in quieting her or obtaining more information, Maria stepped in and led her away to her cottage behind the house. She thought it would be best for Daisy to escape the crowd, and I knew she was right.

Martha tapped me on the shoulder. "The call's for you."

My brain was not working as I shakily took the phone, but I recognized the crisp voice at once.

"Matt, you've got to get back here. The allies have invaded the Normandy coast, the big push has started, and we've got orders to France. It's hell over there. You've got forty-eight hours to get back here before we ship out."

I could only stammer that I understood, and would take the first flight back. This is what we had been waiting for, the chance to put into action all the preparations he and I had been working on. If my brain had not been so jumbled with recent events, I might have asked more questions.

"And also pick up some new stripes. Your promotion to Sergeant just came in."

"Sergeant!" I gasped. It seemed a lofty position.

"Of course," Dr. Mills chuckled. "You don't think I could have a first assistant at a lower rank than Sergeant, do you?" I could almost see the sparkling eyes that marked his sardonic humor.

"And Matt?"

"Yes, sir?"

"I miss you."

R olling and swelling as far as the eye could see, sometimes green but usually reflecting leaden skies, it didn't look much like its sister, the Pacific, that I had known all my life, but it matched my mood. The wind turned the smaller peaks into froth when they dared to protrude into its god-like domain, accentuating my own sense of vulnerability.

Crossing the Atlantic on a troop ship was not my idea of a sea cruise, but it was the only way available. Dr. Mills was furious that his staff could not be flown to Europe and get into the thick of things immediately, but we also had to bring a lot of equipment for setting up aid stations, and the only way to transport everything was by ship. He had flown to England where we would meet him. By this time, the Atlantic was relatively free from German submarines, although the record of sunken transports was dismal in past years.

After the frenetic period of preparation, the trip itself was oppressively quiet. There was plenty of time during the trip to Europe to think about the events that had essentially spoiled my father's wedding day and changed the sleepy Napa Valley forever. As I looked west at the sunset from the fantail of the ship, I thought about my last day at home.

Rev. Antonetti, along with Craig scrambling into the car and Sueann hanging on tenaciously, had roared out of the driveway and onto the highway. After the sports car had disappeared around the bend, some of the neighbors were insistent that we try to follow the fleeing priest with his reluctant passengers in order to resolve all the questions that flooded their minds. Martha, with more presence of mind than most people, had telephoned the police, reporting that Rev. Antonetti was last seen driving north and was in no shape to drive because of having drunk too much. The police didn't seem very interested in that report, but then she mentioned that he had also been accused of rape and that got their attention.

After she hung up we all stood around helplessly, looking at each other and repeating the unbelievable details over and over, shaking our heads. I was particularly concerned for Daisy, whom most of the neighbors did not remember seeing before, but I thought it best to leave her to Maria's tender ministrations for the moment.

"Who is she?" they asked.

"Is she in her right mind?"

"How could she accuse our priest of raping her? When?"

"But why did he run if there is nothing to the accusation?"

"Why did Sueann and Craig go off with him? What's the connection?"

I thought I knew at least most of the answers, but I was not going to volunteer my suspicions until we knew more facts. My father knew me well enough to recognize my reluctance, but I didn't want to give him any details, either.

Less than an hour after making the police report, we received a partial resolution with a telephone call from the police. The expensive convertible had been observed going over a cliff into a ravine off the winding, country road leading to Clear Lake. A man driving a truck, that had barely avoided collision with them just before the accident, reported that the car burst into flames on impact, and there were apparently no survivors. Police reaching the crash site confirmed the finality.

Craig, my first lover, basically a beautiful and caring guy, gone, along with Sueann, still a child, gone, along with her unborn baby. And I suddenly realized we had an orphan upstairs in my bed — my godson, who I realized had a big place in my heart, taking his carefree nap while his parents met their death at the hands of a rapist. I looked up the stairs, realizing that I now had responsibility for him, and there he stood, wearing only his little underpants and still looking a little sleepy, hesitating as he looked down at me, still a stranger. Tears filled my eyes as I raced up the stairs, fearing he might fall in his uncertain state.

I picked him up and pressed him to me, and I guess this startled him because he began to cry. The crying attracted the attention of the group in the living room, and they looked at each other, realizing the added complication of the child for the first time. He also needed changing, I discovered.

Thank god for Martha. She had had two children in her previous marriage, now teenagers, and could automatically step into the breach. Although she capably took over the situation, it was several hours before I remembered the other news, that the new European front had been established and I would have to return to duty immediately. I left on a transcontinental flight the next morning.

It had been my duty to tell Craig's parents about his death, although I had met them only a few times. It was a wrenching experience, although I knew their relationship with Craig, and possibly with Sueann, had not been the best. I thought I should relate to them, at least, my suspicions that little Paul was actually the priest's son. They didn't seem as surprised as I expected, although it was difficult to determine what was in their minds. They seemed a dour pair, little concerned about the fate of the child, and I was secretly pleased that they did not seem anxious to care for Paul. They didn't seem to be the kind of surrogate parents I would select for little Paul.

It was more difficult for Sueann's parents. After the neighbors quietly left, still buzzing from all the excitement, my father and Clarence spent a long time alone and then later included Sueann's mother in their discussion. I hesitated a long time but eventually told my father what I suspected about Paul's real father, and he felt obligated to relate my story to his best friend. Clarence knew that Sueann was smitten with the priest and the appearance of the baby was quite convincing. After all the discussions, influenced to a large extent from what I thought to be a strange aversion on the part of Sueann's mother, it was decided that, for the time being at least, little Paul would remain with my family since I was his godfather. Martha was all smiles about the idea of having a toddler around the house again, and so it was settled, temporarily, at least.

Saying goodbye to Daisy was the hardest part for me, I think. Now that the dam had burst, memories were flooding back to her, each more disturbing than the previous one, it seemed. She clung to me, speaking very little, while I explained what had happened since the confrontation with the priest and her abrupt recollections in our kitchen. I thought she would be relieved to hear that the priest was dead, but that also seemed to add to the burden of sorting out all the details of the past for her. I did not press her for details, nor did I tell her about Paul's confused parentage, thinking that was best left alone. The three sets of parents never discussed the question again, to my knowledge. Maria, and now also Martha, remained Daisy's staunch friends, and I made it clear to my father that I felt responsible for Daisy's future welfare. He offered no argument, and I knew I could rely on him.

I returned to duty in a fog. Throughout all the furious activity at Walter Reed, getting ready for the European duty, my mind was blank, numb, operating on automatic. Even Wes wasn't there to lean on. One of the men said that, while I was at home on furlough, he was transferred to the Pentagon, and another said he had received a commission. None of them knew where to find him, and he had not left any word for me.

When the ship sailed and the American coast had faded behind us, I started to realize that other soldiers on the ship may also be operating under strain that was not peculiar to me. For many it was their first time away from home. They were being rushed to a ferocious war, the new military front that had been discussed in the abstract for so long, to fulfill an obligation that many understood only vaguely. We were leaving family and friends and lovers behind, knowing where we were heading but also knowing that many of us would probably never return (the casualties were reported to be tremendous in France, especially at Omaha Beach). It was rumored that allied forces on the continent would be brought to one million strong, and we were but a tiny segment – to the Generals we were faceless numbers and we knew there was no one to depend on but each other.

I was not alone on the fantail. It had become a favorite place to go to seek the solitude of our thoughts and avoid the crowding of the berthing compartments below-decks. At almost any hour of the day or night, solitary soldiers leaned on unfamiliar ship structures and stared at the water with solemn expressions, remembering, wondering, perhaps regretting something they had done or left undone, reflecting on their lives to that point and realizing that there may be little more of it remaining.

I had another factor to become accustomed to. I was approached repeatedly by soldiers asking me questions relating to our operations, and I realized that now, as a Sergeant, I was expected to know the answers. It was my first experience with rank and responsibility, but three stripes on the sleeve meant authority to many of the

123

soldiers, especially those only recently completing basic training. Usually I had no more information than they did so could not be very helpful, but I realized that, when we arrived on duty, I was going to be expected to give orders and to know what I was doing. This knowledge produced a small spurt of energy that could blank out my own concerns – energy I needed in order to fulfill my role as the Army had decreed. I felt confident of my medical knowledge, but had no experience in the broader scope of command. At Walter Reed I had just been one of the men with ordinary duties to perform.

One night while I was ruminating over these changes in my life and watching the sun set behind us, a corporal came up to me on the fantail and, referring to my name tag, said, "Bristow? Is that Matt Bristow?" When I nodded, he stuck out his hand. "I'm Blake McMann. I'm in your squad – I got to the ship just before it left, but was told I would run into some of Dr. Mills' staff on board, especially a Sergeant Bristow. How ya doing?"

His grip was firm. I also liked his dark eyes that contrasted with his crew-cut red hair and the freckles across his nose. Although about three inches shorter and a few years older, he outweighed me by at least twenty-five pounds, and I could tell it was all muscle.

Blake had had some experience in aid stations before, having spent some time on the African front before being wounded. He pulled up his shirt to show me the long, diagonal scar on his belly that was nearly healed. "Haven't got a spleen anymore," he commented, "but guess I never had much use for it, anyhow." He looked away as if to discourage further discussion of his wounds, and I honored his implicit wish. It must have been more complicated than he implied since he had been flown back to the states for surgery. I told him I would rely on him for advice based on his experience. He flushed like a kid being praised by his coach, the crimson blurring the freckles in the dim light.

"Didn't even get to see my girl before they shipped me back over the pond," he grumbled.

"Yeah, that's tough. I only saw mine for a couple of days before they called me back from furlough." It felt good to refer to Daisy as "my girl."

"What do you know about this Colonel Mills?" he asked. I had thought about how I would respond to that question; now I would get to see how complicated the question — and answer — was.

"I've worked with him in Walter Reed," I answered. "A real pro, and a brilliant surgeon." I tried to keep my face bland.

"Oh, yeah?" He was looking for more.

"He was in charge of the surgical training school there, you know."

"Ah, yes," he said and looked away. I decided my response had passed the test. I noticed he was eying an activity that had been going on ever since night had fallen. I had noticed it but had not commented on it. The door to a spacious room called the rope locker, opening onto the fantail, was the scene of comings and goings of various soldiers, singly and in pairs, although there was no light inside and the rope locker was not really of vital interest to the troops.

"What's going on over there?" Blake wondered.

I grinned. "I think they are getting some R & R already. The hand has its limitations in satisfaction."

Blake looked at me strangely, his imagination apparently clicking over the possibilities I was suggesting. "Shit. . . " he breathed, watching one of the soldiers taking out his cock even before entering the concealing darkness.

He swung back to me. "You going to report them?" he

demanded of his Sergeant.

"Of course not," I stated emphatically. Was this guy going to be trouble?

"But — it's against regulations!" he reminded me persistently. I had to scotch this problem in the bud.

I swung around, practically pinning him to the bulkhead. I must have looked pretty ferocious. "Look, Blake, what's this war all about anyhow? Hatred for anybody who's not like you — Germans hating the Jews, loading them onto trains like cattle, never to be seen again. Germans resenting the Dutch because they broke away from Germany and established their own country 'way back in the 17th century, for God's sake. If guys can have a little happiness, even calling it 'love' for a while, in that dark room, who's to argue about it? Maybe you don't want a blowjob — although I don't know why not — but don't deny others 'love' where they can find it. No one in my section is going to forbid that kind of thing, is that understood?"

I had blurted out that whole speech without taking a breath, and now I felt a little embarrassed. I didn't regret anything I had said, but maybe I was being too hard on the guy without knowing much about him. I was also a little surprised how strongly I felt about the subject, never having put it into words before.

His brown eyes were staring into mine, startled from being exposed to an attitude that he had apparently never encountered before. I admitted to myself that there was some satisfaction in my minor rank after all. I could at least tell my corporal off. I waited for his reaction.

"Yeah, OK, Sarge," he said slowly, searching my face. "I've just never — you know — been in that situation before."

I didn't want to push him, although I had some doubts about his innocence. He was a damn attractive guy, and someone, somewhere, must have expressed interest. I forced myself to smile at him, and he immediately returned the smile, one that lit up his face and almost made me hug him right there. Instead I clapped him on the shoulder. The confrontation was over. Perhaps he just had not understood masculine interest when he had encountered it in the past, or perhaps, like Louisa when I suggested she have sex with men, he just "wasn't interested."

"Besides, it's therapeutic," I continued with only partial irony intended. "When you relieve frustration you avoid tempers flaring, and this long, boring trip will be much calmer without a lot of overwrought testicles."

Again that endearing grin split his face. "Maybe I should try it," he ventured.

"Sure, why not?" I responded, thinking briefly that I wouldn't mind being his partner, but I knew that would not be a good idea because of the complications it might bring. I flashed to Wes for an instant, another lost opportunity. Another situation where this war was limiting my life, I thought.

Blake turned and took a couple of steps toward the door which was empty at the moment. Then he flashed a smile at me over his shoulder and chose the door to the passageway leading to the berthing compartments.

I considered the beckoning door myself for a moment, took a last look over the tossing waves toward home to the west, and took the passageway to my bunk.

* * * * * *

The next evening after eating I went again to the fantail, thinking Blake might be there and we could become better acquainted. A couple of dozen soldiers were there, but Blake wasn't one of them. A small group was playing a dice game near the bulkhead and, as always and at almost any time of the day or night, a few guys were staring out to sea, thinking their private thoughts. One private was leaning against a gun mount, apparently watching the game but something about him caught my eye. His expression was solemn, almost downcast, but the reason was not apparent.

While my thoughts were on home, from time to time my eyes drifted back to the dejected private. Occasionally he looked around the ship but his attention always returned to watching the game. My curiosity overcame my reluctance to break into his reverie, and I approached him with a friendly attitude.

"Looks like the weather might clear up, with that bright red sunset to the west," I started.

The soldier looked up at me as if waking from a dream. "Huh? Oh, yeah. . . "

"What's the old saying? 'Red sky at night, sailor's delight'?" I persisted.

He roused himself, realizing that I was not going to go away and leave him alone that easily. "Yeah, I guess that's right. . . 'Red sky in morning, sailors take warning.' Haven't heard that since I was a kid on the farm." He was warming to me, slowly.

"Where was the farm?" I asked, settling in next to him at the gun mount so he had to turn away from the game in progress to talk to me.

"Iowa." I wasn't being very effective in distracting him. He turned again toward the game.

"You like dice games?" I wasn't going to give up that easily.

He returned to me a little sheepishly, and said, "Not really." I noticed his eyes drop to my medic insignia and study it for a moment, and then rise to my face. "Not really the game."

This was going to be more difficult than I had thought, but instinct put the words in my mouth. "One of the players?"

There was no immediate answer. He was tall, thin, and rangy, with blue eyes and sandy hair with a receding hairline, although he didn't appear older than twenty-four or -five. By this time in the Army, having met many like him, I could almost bet on his general background – a draftee with a professional education, not suitable or interested in an officer's rank, thrown into the mixture of gun-carrying toughs some called "cannon-fodder" for the duration. If they survived they would return to their civilian jobs in banks or offices as soon as the war was over, perhaps scarred by it but trying to forget the bad parts. For some of them it was the first time they had really been exposed to realities of life away from their protected homes, parents, and wives.

To test my intuition, I took a stab in the dark, crooking my neck at him. "Let's see, you're a – an insurance salesman?"

"No," he chuckled. At least I had his attention. "A high school English teacher."

"Ah. In Iowa?"

"Yep."

"Married?"

"Yep, two years."

"Uh huh." Now where do I go, I asked myself? "They call you 'Iowa'?" It was common to take the nickname of your home state, especially when with a group of men with origins scattered throughout the States.

"Uh huh."

"And you have a problem with one of the guys?"

He looked at me and again at my caduceus, but then looked away. "Look, Sarge," he muttered. "I know you're a medic and all, but I don't think you'd understand."

I should have nodded and walked away, but having come this far, I decided to make another try. "I'd be happy to try, if you want me to." I said it in a low, soothing tone, trying to invite his confidence. It paid off. His gaze returned to the game.

"It's Nebraska."

Nebraska? "Nebraska?"

He sighed, still turned away. "See the real handsome guy, the one shaking the dice in his hands right now?" It was easy to identify his problem — an athletic-appearing soldier apparently engrossed in the game. Husky and crew-cut, his biceps bulged from his rolled sleeves as he moved his hands; his thighs stretched his fatigues as he knelt, noisily participating in a most masculine pursuit with others like him, cursing and chortling depending on the luck of the toss, apparently completely at ease with his rough buddies. His broad shoulders were meant for football, it seemed; his nose was twisted a little to give his face a roguish appearance, which may have resulted from some injury on the gridiron. He was undoubtedly a handsome, rugged specimen.

"That's 'Nebraska'?"

"Uh huh. He was a high school athletic coach."

Where do I go from here? Why did I ever get into this situation anyway?

"Well, there's only a river between you." It was a poor try at levity, but he turned toward me again with a grin on his face. It turned his angular face into one of amused but appealing intensity; he should try it more often, I thought.

"There's more between us than the Missouri River, I'm afraid." I could tell he was choosing his words carefully. "And what's more, I don't understand any of it."

I knew now what the problem was, but I had a very poor

idea of how to arrive at a solution. But "Iowa" was looking at me and rightly so, having bared his soul to show his complicated burden, and it was my responsibility to handle it.

"Does he know how you feel?"

He shook his head. "When I try to talk to him he starts talking about ball scores or how the war is going. I want to talk seriously, but he avoids touchy subjects. And even if we could talk, I keep wondering why I'm mooning over him anyway. I mean, I've got a wife at home, whom I love very much, so why am I going through all this?" His voice was urgent and the hang-dog expression had returned. His agony was evident to me, but understanding it and doing something to relieve it were two different things.

I had noticed that "Nebraska" had glanced our way several times from his squat in the game, whenever "Iowa" wasn't looking his way. It was obvious to me that he was observing us talking together with more than casual interest.

"Have you considered that maybe he is as afraid to open up to you as you are afraid to be truthful with him?"

He stared at me for a moment. "Truthful? What do you mean?"

Again I paused, trying to find the right words. "Look, it's no crime nor even unusual to want affection, even sex, from men even though you are happily married, especially under these conditions. Why does everyone assume that we must make choices between women and men as sex partners?"

I looked at the tossing waves, trying to put my beliefs into words. "I don't think interest in men is being unfair to the wife, but you are being dishonest with yourself if you refuse to face reality. One doesn't necessarily exclude the other. It's the same with many of us – including me."

"Iowa" studied my face, perhaps doubting my sincerity,

131

but waiting for me to continue. By this time it was almost pitch dark on the fantail, and the activity had picked up in the rope locker. It was too dark for the crap shooters to see their game, and the group was breaking up. I noticed "Nebraska" dawdled behind, however, leaning on the rail on the starboard side, looking thoughtfully down at the water. It occurred to me that he might be gathering courage to go into the rope locker. I had other ideas.

"Wait here for me, huh? I'll be back in a minute," I said. "Iowa" may have suspected I was giving an excuse for escaping from an uncomfortable situation, but he nodded. He looked again toward the game but saw the area empty. He probably assumed that "Nebraska" had gone to his bunk. He turned again to the rail as if hypnotized by our frothy wake. I crossed over to a point near the unsuspecting athlete, close enough to talk, but I didn't have to begin. He started the conversation.

"You a friend of 'Iowa's'?" His voice was husky and vibrant, and I suspected he could bellow the full length of a football field with no question of being heard. But he wasn't bellowing now.

"Not, not really. Just met him."

"Seems a nice guy."

"He thinks the same about you, except – "

He looked closely at me in the darkness. "Huh?"

"He says you don't talk much."

"Huh?" Obviously this guy was not an intellectual genius.

"At least not about the more important things."

"Yeah? Like what?"

"Oh," I appeared to toss off a few subjects casually, "friendship, companionship, sex – that sort of thing."

"Sex? He wants to talk about sex?"

132

"Doesn't everybody?" I smiled. We both looked across the fantail at the tall figure slumped near the rail. He looked lonely and vulnerable indeed at that moment. I could almost hear the gears turning in the athlete's head.

"Well," I decided abruptly, and hoping I had sown the seed properly, "guess I'll see what's up in the rope locker tonight." "Nebraska" looked sharply at me, but I walked away and through the beckoning door, into the darkness of groping hands, rigid cocks, and welcoming mouths.

I forgot about "Iowa" and "Nebraska" for a while; it was fully a half-hour later that I emerged, drained of most of my frustrations, and noticed two figures stretched out on the deck near the rail. In itself that would not have aroused much interest, except that this time, one figure was on top of the other and they were talking, murmuring, actually, face to face, very closely indeed. Although they appeared to be fully clothed, I was pretty sure they were talking about sex, and "Iowa" was on top.

16

I saw very little of England. Col. Mills was waiting for us at the dock, and we spent two days supervising the unloading of our supplies and transferring them to landing craft. The next day we crossed the channel uneventfully, landing at the devastated Omaha Beach and picked our way between shell craters to solid ground. Here and there were splotches of blood left behind by Americans caught by the horrendous fire power of the defenders. When our supplies were landed, we moved inland to catch up with the action, Dr. Mills in the vanguard. Our first primary aid station was actually constructed near Cherbourg, a port that would be important for incoming supplies and troops. The casualties started flooding in even before we were completely set up, before we had the big red-cross flag flying.

Blake was enthusiastic about the preparations and organization of the aid station as designed by Dr. Mills, but I had nothing to compare it with. All I knew were the hundreds of bodies, some more dead than alive, that were carried, driven, or dragged into our station. There were three surgeons attached to our station in addition to Dr. Mills, and they worked almost around the clock, day after day, trying to breathe life into some of those actually beyond saving, and patching up the devastated heads, legs, arms, and torsos split by bullets and shell fragments. Soon it was all a blur, my days and nights reduced to making quick decisions as to salvageable or hopeless and then trying to decide which should be treated first.

Soon it was routine for me, and sometimes for Blake and others with special surgical training, to handle the relatively simple cases ourselves, since the surgeons were obviously too busy to spend time with the easier cases. The younger doctors were generally novices at field medicine, but their exposure to the battle trauma added years of surgical experience in a few weeks in the aid station. The nurses also worked until they were ready to drop, but they relied heavily on us medics for most of the routine care. Looking back on those long days, it seems remarkable that we were able to save as many as we did. The only aspect that worked in our favor was that most of the soldiers were strong and healthy to begin with and could withstand an enormous amount of physical damage before actually succumbing to their injuries.

The Canadian and English forces were still frustrated in their progress around the Orne River to the north of us, with Caen as their primary target. Toward the middle of July, there was a lull in the fighting for us. We found we could actually sleep for a few hours between onslaughts, but then it was time to move the station closer to the lines of fighting and start all over again. Usually the aid stations operated on a skip-and-jump schedule, one farther behind the lines moved to the forefront as the battle lines changed. Dr. Mills was always there, always ready with an answer to a seemingly impossible question, medical or logistic.

I recalled visiting with Reba Mills the night before our departure for Europe. Dr. Mills had already left for England, and she invited me to their house; I had no idea what the purpose was, but I had grown very fond of her and wanted to help her if I could. When I arrived she gathered me into her arms and held me for a long time, almost as if I was a substitute for her husband. Then she collected herself and talked very frankly. It was my impression that she had maintained a courageous front for her husband, but when he was gone she lost much of her courage.

"Please, Matt, take care of my husband for me, will

135

you?"

I tried to smile reassuringly, but am not sure I succeeded. "I was thinking that he was going to take care of me!" I responded.

She smiled wanly. "I know him all too well. He will work too hard, make too many sacrifices, just because he knows it will help someone, until it's too late."

I nodded, knowing she was right.

"And Matt — I know he — likes you — no, more — he needs you, someone with your — sensitivity. You can help him more than I ever could."

For the first time I realized that she knew and understood the masculine links between her husband and me. She not only knew but approved of our sexual relationship, and she was telling me that it was all right because it was good for her husband. When I left the house, I didn't feel like a substitute wife but as a special lover with a special mission. I never mentioned that meeting to Dr. Mills, but I didn't have to; I think he understood it all ready.

There was little time for love for us, but if I happened to be asleep in my tent when he decided he could afford a few hours of sleep, he sometimes kissed me awake. Our sex was more mutual than it had been in Washington. I know he needed me as much as I needed him. Blake soon grew accustomed to looking for him in my tent, asleep in my bunk, if he could not find him in the command tent, and no questions were asked. I was aware of Blake's eyes focused on me sometimes when I was involved in other things. There were questions there — and something else.

Although it was not a total stranger to me during my experience at Walter Reed, death became a constant companion in France. Bodies were brought to us that obviously were only a tangled mass of blood and tissue, but the medic could not bring himself to leave him in the field.

We understood. We handled it. Sometimes we were rewarded with near miracles, able to save massively injured soldiers with quick intervention made routine through Dr. Mills' approach to care. The fact that these soldiers were prime, healthy specimens was an important factor on our side.

When we could, Dr. Mills and I would make rounds, usually by flashlight late at night just before catching some sleep. The patients were on rows of cots separated only by canvas curtains, and we tried to be quiet to avoid waking those who were able to sleep. Sometimes one of the nurses or other doctors would accompany us, but more frequently they were too fatigued or were caring for the more acute cases.

One aspect that concerned us about the organization was the unreliability and timeliness of evacuation of patients who were in recovery and should be removed from the constant emergency situation of the primary aid station. They needed more nursing care than surgery, and we were ill-equipped to provide it. Such a patient was Buck, a gunner who had been severely injured by a blast close to his emplacement; the gun had shielded his torso, but both legs and arms were riddled with bullets and shell fragments. On rounds one night, we found him draped professionally but grotesquely, both legs stretched out in traction and both arms in casts. Dr. Mills and I checked him over and decided he did not need particular attention, but I noticed tears running down his cheeks. I bent close and encouraged him to talk.

"You'll just think I'm a fuckin' baby," he responded reluctantly.

"That's one thing nobody will ever accuse you of, Buck," I answered quietly. "You need more pain-killers? Tell us the problem." His face showed a few scratches from flying debris, but it was obvious he was just a handsome kid,

137

perhaps eighteen or nineteen, who should have been on the baseball diamond at home.

He shook his head. "No, I ain't got too much pain now, but – maybe that's the problem. There's time to think more and – "

"Yeah, about what?" I inquired. Dr. Mills had remained quiet, allowing me to do the inquiring.

"After all this shit, gettin' blasted and laid up like this, I mean, I got a fuckin' hardon that won't quit! After all this, I got a case of lover's nuts and how!" He chortled at the incongruity of it.

Dr. Mills reached across his body and wrapped his hand around a solid tube-shape distending the drape. "Hey, that's a good sign," he said. "Shows you're on the recovery road!"

"Yeah, I suppose so," Buck groaned, "but with both arms in casts I can't do anything about it! And it's killing me!"

Dr. Mills and I looked at each other for a moment, and then he bent and whispered in Buck's ear, "You're in luck. The Sarge here is just great at tender, loving care. He can take care of your problem in no time." He pulled the canvas all the way around the cot and, giving me a little grin, left us alone.

I pulled back the drape covering his abdomen, exposing a very randy hardon that throbbed high and handsome. When my fist went around it, he groaned. When I began to move my hand up and down, he gasped and stiffened. When I took it in my mouth he moaned as if in pain, but when I stole a glance at his face I knew he was definitely not in pain. It was only a moment later that his dam burst and flooded me, leaving him gasping. When I looked again his face wore a beatific smile of gratitude. By the time I replaced his covering and pulled aside the curtains again, he was asleep. I chalked the treatment up to instant therapeutic success. At that point I was the one with a demanding erection.

From time to time a quiet period allowed us to relax a little from the 24-hour schedule, and we could explore the countryside, the bombed-out villages and crater-pocked fields registering as future memories of the devastation of war. It was rumored that the allies were grouping for an all-out assault at some point on the German lines, but during the lull we could have our recovering patients returned to more comprehensive care facilities. One day Blake and I decided to check out a jeep and take a little trip around the liberated territory nearby.

The grass in the fields was startlingly green but unkempt, of course, and marred by large shell craters and toppled remnants of buildings. Islands of untouched habitation remained, but one time a seemingly intact house turned out to be only a facade, with the majority of the house reduced to shatters behind the intact front. A few civilians were visible, scratching among the ruins, sometimes accompanied by the family dog that had miraculously survived. The roads were pitted and torn by tracks of tanks and armored vehicles, but navigable between hedgerows of trees. Remnants of apple orchards dangled green fruit, valiant in their survival. This was called the "box country" because of the depressed roads between rows of trees near Villiers-Bocage. It had been won with heavy casualties, as we knew only too well.

Although "home" had become a faded fantasy for all of us, it was possible to at least come close to forgetting the pain and death in which we existed, and pretend we were enjoying an uncomplicated drive through the summer countryside dotted with tattered wildflowers. Just when we could settle back in contentment, more of Gen. Bradley's bombers would fly over, either from English bases or from captured air fields in Normandy, aiming for wholesale destruction of another designated site – and also destroying our illusion.

After about a half-hour of meandering in the neighboring vicinity, Blake pointed out figures on the roadside in the distance; we couldn't tell who they were but they were unlikely to be threatening, we knew. As we came closer the figures appeared to be two young girls, far from any houses that we could see. They wore simple dresses that looked as though they had seen better days.

As we approached them they waved at us and we could see they were laughing and giggling, as if out for a walk on a balmy day. Blake brought the jeep to a stop beside them and they immediately started talking to us, obviously not in any danger or trouble. Of course we could not understand a word they were saying, but they were smiling and blushing, and poking each other as if making risque conversation. They made motions that clearly meant they would like us to take them somewhere down the road.

"That one with the big comb in her hair is really a beauty, isn't she?" Blake commented.

"Yeah, but I like the blond one better," I answered. "How old do you think they are — eighteen?"

"Yeah, I would think so. What do you suppose they want?"

"Why didn't I take French in school as my advisor suggested?" I grumbled. At least I had had a smattering of German, and that might come in handy one day.

"They want a ride, that's for sure," Blake decided.

"Ride where?"

He shrugged and decided to try sign language. He pointed to them and then to the road ahead, and they nodded enthusiastically. Without another word they climbed up on the jeep behind us, and we started off to wherever the road led, the girls giggling and laughing, their hair flying in the warm breeze. What a rotten youth these

140

girls must have had, four years of occupation by the Wehrmacht, I thought. Perhaps even sexual violence.

"It seems almost as if we are back home, taking a joy ride in the country with our girl friends," Blake grinned. I hadn't seen him so relaxed in weeks. Then I felt a hand reach over my shoulder and slip between the buttons of my shirt. The sly fingers touched one of my nipples and began to play with it, the girl's chin resting on my shoulder.

Blake smiled at me, watching wide-eyed. I was trying to decide if this could be a trap of some sort, but then she started to nibble at my ear and I decided that it was nothing more nor less than normal flirtation. The other girl was watching also, and when I did not object to the attention, she started plying her wiles with Blake. My groin grew tight; it was the first female contact I had had in many weeks.

As we cruised down the abandoned highway, the girls became more and more aggressive. I didn't really mind but they didn't make Blake's job of dodging potholes any easier. Then one of the girls pointed toward a large structure on the hillside nearby and, tapping on Blake's shoulder, urged him to turn off the road. There was a long driveway up the hill, ending in an old church, black with age but with most of the stained glass windows still intact. The roof, however, had largely collapsed toward the rear of the building. We could see that the old bell was still in the tower, but had fallen to the floor of its chamber. If there had been a cross on top, it had disappeared.

The girls immediately jumped out and started for the church when Blake stopped in front. "Think it's a trap?" Blake asked. There was no sign of life inside or outside. I shrugged. Blake reached under the seat and extracted a pistol that he had hidden there. We were actually not allowed to carry firearms when at work, but there was no prohibition at other times. The girls shied when they saw

141

the gun but made soothing noises and beckoned us into the old church, only mildly subdued.

Cautiously we pulled open the heavy door and entered the vestibule of the church which was floored with flagstones centuries old. Yellowed paint was peeling from the rear wall of the sanctuary, turned orange from the sunlight through the red-paned windows. Ahead was a graceful archway leading to the rows of pews for the worshippers. When we moved into the auditorium further we could look up at the sky, deep blue with white, scudding clouds drifting east, through the remnants of the roof where only broken, black spars remained. There was nothing left in the depths of the church except a high podium where the priest must have presided on Sundays, exhorting his flock to good deeds and loving their neighbors. The windows had once pictured revered figures in stained glass, but panes were missing in vital spots which gave them a moth-eaten appearance.

After reviewing the building thoroughly, there didn't appear to be any places of concealment and Blake slipped the pistol into his pocket. At first the girls were uncertain and shy, perhaps awed by the presence of religious spirits of the past, but that soon faded. They each took a seat in the last pew, one on each side, and Blake and I followed their lead. The blond girl started caressing my thigh and it wasn't long before I drew her close and kissed her gently. She fluttered in my arms like a grounded bird, and her breathing quickened. She needed me to release her earth-bound ties, to send her aloft to fly freely as all birds are meant to do.

When I moved one hand under her dress to cup her budding breast she moaned and leaned back so I could lower the garment. Her nipples were tense, and begged for my lips. She was already moist between her legs, dampening my exploring fingertips.

Behind the pews and down the central aisle, the floor

142

was carpeted, sculptured deep red, rain-stained and none too clean, and that's where we ended up, couples side by side. While not virginal, the girls were obviously starved for affection and not hesitant to show their desire. Perhaps they thought of us as gallant saviors, the modern equivalent of knights riding in on our trusty jeep-steed, and it was their pleasure to sacrifice their virtue to the conquering heroes, or at least that's what I imagined. My metaphors were crowding my brain.

Each action I took brought an even greater reaction. I quickly realized that she was also responding to sounds and words of her friend. Each little squeal from the dark-haired girl immediately brought a heightened response in my partner and vice versa, suggesting that the two girls' relationship was not entirely devoid of mutual passion.

What they did not grasp was the significance of Blake and me performing side by side, only inches apart, which was almost as exciting as the obvious coupling. His buttocks, trim and rounded, thrusting rhythmically as his eyes met mine; his firmness straight and strong, matching mine stroke for stroke, set off by his bright red pubic curls; our simultaneous cresting — too soon, much too soon — that revealed a hidden scenario that would not be acknowledged.

When Blake and I slumped, temporarily exhausted, at their sides the girls shifted attentions to each other, avid for further ecstacies as we watched. Blake continued with his hand, but he was also watching me, still with my pants around my feet, while I was watching them, and surprisingly he crested again that way within minutes. I could have entered his fantasy, but something held me back. The girls ignored us.

The sun was dropping steadily lower, and after a few minutes I tapped my girl on the shoulder, making signs that we should leave. They took the suggestion in good humor,

143

but I had the impression that this was neither the first nor the last times for their shared passions. As we left the shattered building-relic, Blake turned back, dropped to one knee, and genuflected in the direction of what once had been the altar. I didn't inquire whether he was asking for forgiveness or expressing gratitude.

When we finally persuaded the girls to climb back in the jeep for the return trip, they chattered and caressed each other, apparently oblivious to us, all the way to the village we had passed through. They waved briefly at us as we drove off.

"Do you get the idea that we may have been used, just a little?" I asked Blake.

"Sure do, but who cares? I enjoyed it — didn't you?" I grinned at him, not sure which parts of it I had enjoyed most. I suppose we had also used them, to some extent. Maybe it was always that way. . .

As we drove into the aid station, Dr. Mills hailed us from the command tent. "The allies have broken through the German lines at Avranches, and it's time to move again. We're on the road to Paris!"

17

The location for the new aid station was not the best, I thought. The crew that set it up tried to use some remaining buildings, actually they were shacks with corrugated metal roofs, to save time and materials. When the August sun beat down on those metal roofs, everybody was overheated and edgy, to say the least. As the medic in charge of installation, I could have objected, could have required them to set us up in the usual tents. But I decided that there was no time for that because wounded were being brought in even before we had completely set up, and we went to full speed immediately. We were so close to the front that the sounds of shells landing and exploding on our forces were startling, louder than usual.

To say that there was a break-through was a little exaggerated. The enemy was deeply entrenched and resisted stubbornly, and our casualties mounted as the days flew by. A relatively quiet day could be followed by a horrendous influx of patients the next day; the battle line did not change much from day to day. Avranches was the so-called gateway to the Brittany plains and then to Paris, we hoped.

Some of the company commanders in the field began sending a few of the more fatigued soldiers back to the aid station in order to get a night's sleep occasionally. They never interfered with our activities, but almost every night there were a few single tents or bed rolls around the periphery of the station. We called them "R & R" tents, although they certainly weren't for the usual "Rest and Relaxation." In the morning they were always gone – the

145

men returned to their units after a night's sleep.

One day about dawn, after snatching a couple of hours sleep, I was abruptly startled awake in my tent by the sudden stripping away of my covering blanket.

"Sergeant! On your feet!"

My bleary eyes finally focused on Capt. Hollister, the senior nurse in the station. She was a rather plain, bony woman with brown hair and eyes and almost no breasts, but a good nurse and one noted for being a stickler for regulations. I raised my head wearily, and then noticed that my morning erection was not nearly so fatigued. Since I always slept nude, it nodded tensely in full view at her interruption. Her eyes fell to it for a long moment, and then returned to me accusingly.

"On your feet, I said!"

It took me a few seconds to marshall my wits and stand up for the officer. My erection was already very much awake. Her eyes snapped at mine in the dim dawn light.

"There is a rumor around the station that you are having sex with patients from time to time. That must mean that you are — like that. Is there any truth to that?"

"Like that?" I repeated, stalling for time. Dr. Mills had suggested a second time that I use my TLC on a needy soldier, and I had serviced a few more when they had deliberately suggested or requested it. Was she suggesting I was "attacking" or raping soldiers? If I told her that the Colonel had suggested it, would that cause trouble for him? Why couldn't people mind their own business, I wondered.

"Yes, you know — queer! Even if the soldier asks for such unthinkable actions, it is against regulations as you know very well! Monstrous!"

I took a step closer to her and her eyes narrowed. Another step, my erection preceding me by its rather considerable length. Her eyes dropped again to it, and

146

misted over; she seemed to be remembering some previous, pleasant occasion with such an instrument. And even though her entrance had been traumatic, I had to admit she was a desirable woman, especially since she was the first one in many weeks who had even looked at my nudity, not counting the two French girls in the church.

My voice dropped to what I hoped was a sultry level. "Do I look like some monster, Captain?"

A line of perspiration was breaking out on her upper lip, and her fingers began to tremble. Still staring at the bobbing length, she answered, "It certainly is big and – "

I moved closer, beginning to stroke her hair. She quivered perceptibly. The poor woman was starved for sex. When her eyes rose they were moist, but she did not move away. She searched my eyes and I could see her original virtuous demand for discipline fading under the reality of the moment. She made a little gulp, and that is all I needed to take her into my arms. In the back of my mind was the thought that I might just be adding to my troubles, since fraternization of officers with enlisted men was also very much against regulations.

She would not have been my first choice for a sex partner, but she was warm and receptive in my arms. Her small breasts, surprisingly firm and peaking in the loose scrub dress, pressed against my naked chest. I had not smelled a woman's perfumed body for a long time, and I throbbed even more enthusiastically. After a quivering moment in my arms, her hand dropped to grasp me and it jerked strongly in her fist. Immediately she squealed and tensed, and I wondered if she had had an orgasm merely from that contact.

Before she left she had at least three more that I was aware of, one more than I did. After adjusting her clothes and patting her hair more or less in place, she attempted to regain her composure, her position as a superior officer,

147

with only partial success.

"Well – obviously you're not – like that!" she murmured. "I – uh – will see you at breakfast, I suppose?" I nodded, but held my smile until after she had left the tent. Only time would tell what the future might hold for us.

That was a bad day (among many bad days) at the station. The sounds of shelling seemed louder than at some times in the past few days, and we could only assume that there was little progress in the battles raging nearby. Low clouds had apparently precluded the bombing runs that usually roared overhead several times each day.

There was no moon that night. I had just finished my late night rounds and was heading back to my tent when I encountered a soldier on the path, apparently not part of the staff. He didn't seem to be injured. I saw him glance at my name taped to my scrub shirt, and then he caught my arm to stop me. He looked closer in the darkness at the name scribbled on adhesive tape and then at my face. "Bristow? You Sergeant Bristow, the medic I've heard about?"

I was nearly dead on my feet and the last thing I needed was to be accosted by another Sergeant over some petty complaint, I thought. My response was grumpy. "I think I'm the only Sergeant Bristow around here."

He ignored my curt reply. "I hear you give great blow jobs." He didn't smile nor mince words. Apparently I was getting a reputation. Indeed there must be rumors as mentioned by Captain Hollister, and either he wanted in on the action or to pick a fight. He was a handsome, strapping guy and, despite my fatigue, my hormones were responsive to him. If he were like most of the guys, it would only take a minute or two to solve the problem. I sighed a little and my hand dropped to his crotch, gripping a sizable mound.

"Not so fast, Sergeant," he growled, gripping my wrist. My fatigue reasserted itself. Is this some disgruntled morality purge, I wondered? I really needed some sleep. His eyes had grown piercing, and they held mine insistently.

"You can have that only if I can have yours," he stated unequivocally.

"Huh?" I was too fatigued to think very clearly at the moment. I noticed he had not removed my hand, but was actually pressing it against his growing bulge. I stared at him stupidly.

"Look, Sarge," he growled. "It's been months since I had sex with a guy, ever since we landed at Omaha Beach and even before that. I dream about it all the time – when there's a chance to sleep." He glanced at my crotch which was totally unrevealing in my loose scrub pants. "You're not just a one-way guy, are you?"

I shook my head, not really believing my ears. When he reached for me I realized that I was already responding without being consciously aware of it, and his touch was enough to start the juices flowing. His grip became almost painfully strong, and I could see a new tension in his face.

"Come on, Bristow," he pulled me closer to him. "I got a tent on the other side of that shack. What do you say we get naked?" Before I realized it I was walking beside him toward the R & R tents, his arm wrapped possessively around my shoulder.

It became clear that night that even the heaviest fatigue can be replaced with the headiest sexuality under the right conditions, at least for a while. We "plugged into" each other and remained that way, in and out of orgasmic waves, for several hours in his minuscule tent. He was alternately gentle and demanding, and I found myself responding immediately to his pressures with total abandon and total enjoyment.

149

I don't know when we finally fell asleep in exhaustion, but we were awakened by the deafening crash of a mortar shell exploding almost on top of us. The enemy must have gotten our range, and were determined to wipe out our aid station in total disregard for all Geneva Convention rules, of course.

Clasped as we were in each other's arms, there was a mad scramble to disentangle ourselves and pull on some clothes. In the melee the tent went down around us, but we shook it off and I ran to the main treatment shack that was still trembling from the shock. At almost the same time, Col. Mills arrived wearing only his shorts, shouting something indistinguishable.

At that moment we heard the whistle of another incoming shell, and darted behind a jeep that was parked nearby. The shell exploded the building only yards away from us in a blinding flash, scattering the boards, the corrugated roof sheets, and patients' bodies in pieces in all directions. Some of the debris struck the jeep, blasting it to a tangled mass of steel, but miraculously I was struck only a glancing blow by a falling timber. I felt the breeze of one of the roof panels whirling by.

As the rain of debris quieted, I turned to Dr. Mills, my brain in turmoil, but his head was missing, amputated efficiently by one of the metal sheets that had roofed the station. What I remember seeing was blood spurting from the arteries in his neck and his dog tag chain still in place around the stump. It was several seconds before his body crumpled to the ground at my feet.

*   *   *   *   *   *

On August 25th I drove a jeep through the streets of Paris to the cheers and shouts of the populace, but it was Blake at my side rather than Dr. Mills, as I had always envisioned. The happy scene was blurred by the tears in my eyes.

18

We had received some rather unusual communications from Army headquarters before entering Paris. All the remaining officers (Captain Hollister had been killed in the direct hit) had been transferred to stations in southern France, near Marseilles and Toulon in the Rhône valley, where a new offensive was underway, but Blake and I, along with several other medics, were assigned to temporary duty in or near Paris. Our purpose was to set up an aid station in existing buildings to serve the residents on a temporary basis until pre-war clinic and hospital facilities could be reorganized.

Our little squad was assigned the area on the fringe of the city near the Château de Vincennes, and we were to make Charenton our headquarters. Perhaps it was the communications links that were fragmentary in many areas that entered into that selection process. We had to drive almost all the way through Paris before finding our assigned area.

Although Paris was obviously very old, it did not appear damaged from the war very much. No one, not even the Germans, had wanted to destroy the city. The Parisians crowded the streets or hung out of upper floor windows as the allies marched (or more correctly wandered) through the city. Some of the streets were very narrow and winding while some were unusually wide with esplanades down the middle. Above all the atmosphere was joy at being liberated.

Everyone was kissing everyone else, it seemed. Women of all descriptions, and even some of the men, were trying to kiss the soldiers. At first the Americans avoided the men's grasps, but some of the bystanders passed jugs of wine to the soldiers and soon one pair of lips was just like another. We were closer to celebrating guests than liberators, it seemed.

One of the soldiers in my unit had salvaged a camera and was taking pictures of us and the streets filled with people. Those pictures would be considered remarkable one day, I guessed.

"I hear that the Parisians were just as happy in greeting Marshall Pétain less than a week ago," Blake grumbled. "He was the leader of the collaboration, you know." A girl tried to climb aboard the jeep, but Blake pushed her off impatiently. "And why did they put the French General DeLattre de Tassigny and his troops first in the liberation procession? What did they do, for Christ's sake?"

Blake's grumbling did little to help me in my grieving for Dr. Mills. I didn't actually realize how much I loved the man until he was dead. Maybe he knew, even if I didn't. The letter to Reba Mills in Washington was the most difficult job I had ever had, and going through his remaining effects to send back to her was performed in a torrent of tears. God knows I hadn't taken care of him as she had asked me to, but I knew he would have enjoyed this day and our procession through Paris, and I tried to capture the spirit of the occasion for his memory's sake. And we still had a job to do, although setting up a clinic in Paris was not my idea of furthering the defeat of the Wehrmacht very much.

Our underground contact was known only by the code name of "Erik," which I thought was rather obvious, whose address was on Gambetta Boulevard in a suburb called Charenton. We were to proceed to that address and receive instructions from Erik. There was also a rather enigmatic postscript to the effect that all Paris groups were to try to

153

locate a Professor von Osterhaus and notify the Pentagon of his whereabouts. That name seemed to strike a bell in my mind, but I didn't remember where I had heard it.

Blake had studied French in high school, and also done some reading on the culture. He continued to amaze me by his scope of knowledge about seemingly diverse things, but he was a good assistant to have along. I wasn't going to be able to use the smattering of Spanish I had picked up from the workers at home, nor would the fragmentary German I remembered from school be very helpful, it would seem.

"Charenton is very famous in some circles, you know," he mentioned as we drove through it, looking for Gambetta Boulevard. At my quizzical look, he added, "This was where the Marquis de Sade was imprisoned in a mental hospital."

"Who's that?" I asked innocently. I only vaguely remembered hearing the name somewhere.

"A famous nobleman who explored some pretty extreme ideas about sex, combining beatings and whippings and torture with sex. That's where we get our word, 'sadism'."

"Oh?" I answered, only half concentrating. "Was he a big torturer, then?"

"Some say he liked pain both ways, to give it and take it, because it increased sexual pleasure. He claimed that everybody had some tendencies along those lines."

"Hmmm – oh, there it is!" Gambetta was a beautiful street just off the main thoroughfare; the buildings had tree-shaded gardens in front, some with small fountains and with low stone walls and fancy gates. Most of the houses appeared vacant. The address we sought was almost immediately apparent, and we walked through the neglected garden, up the winding stone pathway to a huge entry door. The sound of the heavy knocker echoed through the tall structure.

154

After a moment the door was opened by a young dark-haired girl in a black dress and frilly white apron. She murmured, "Bonjour?"

I realized that this was not going to be easy because of the language problem. I looked at Blake, but he didn't seem to be ready to provide any conversation in French. I stammered, "We – are – here – to talk to – Erik."

Her face was a picture of puzzlement until I said the word "Erik." "Ah, Erik!" she said, and moved back, motioning us to follow. She led the way to a huge, sculptured door only a few feet from the entrance and opened it. She chattered a few words to someone inside, and in a moment the door was opened widely by a slim, dark-haired man with a tight smile.

"Did someone ask for Erik?" I was relieved to hear words in English.

"We were told that Erik could assist us. We are here to set up a local clinic as part of the liberation operation." I didn't know how much he knew about our orders. Our uniforms certainly identified us.

"Ah yes, the Americans. I am Erik." The voice was low and musical, and his dark eyes scrutinized us closely before we invited us in. The pretty maid was peeking at us curiously from a door down the hall, but she quickly disappeared, blushing shyly, when she saw me looking at her.

It was an impressive home, with ceilings probably twelve feet high and doors at least ten feet in scale, all carved in gold and ivory with heavy gold fittings. Erik ushered us into a sort of combined dining room and library where a large fireplace with marble mantle dominated one wall. A large window opened onto the garden, its lush growth adding grace to the room. He showed us to handsome chairs placed on an obviously expensive oriental rug in front of an ancient wall tapestry. I hesitated to sink into the chairs' plush comfort in fear that I might soil them.

"Please accept my gratitude for driving the Germans out of Paris," our host said carefully. His dark eyes seemed to see everything at once, flickering occasionally to Blake but apparently recognizing that I was in charge. His dark hair was cropped short on his head, and more of it showed prominently above the neck of his ivory-colored silk shirt; when he moved it was with feline grace. Perhaps that impression was enhanced by the thin, expensive trousers that accentuated his trim buttocks and a long, slim bulge extending down one of his unusually long legs. The over-all impression was one of wealth but also of concealed power, a power with which he was born.

"Paris has been one of our goals for many months," I replied, not wishing to promote a discussion of the war but uneasy about accomplishing our errand too abruptly. "I understand you were involved in the underground?"

He shrugged expressively but ignored the question. I probably shouldn't have mentioned that, I realized. His face remained cool, almost rigidly composed, as he spoke. "If I can help you, I will be only too happy."

"We were told that you could help in setting up the clinic."

"Ah, oui, yes," he nodded. "I believe you will find the building near by satisfactory for your purposes. Come, I will show you."

Down the street and around the corner was a large building that had been used as a parking garage at one time and was now vacant. I forced myself to avoid watching his entrancing rear as he led us up the inclined ramp to the first level of the large structure.

The lighting was poor but there was plenty of space, and the electricity was working. Blake agreed that the building

156

could be used without too many problems, and the sloping driveways would be convenient to wheel equipment and patients in and out of the treatment spaces. I could see that Blake was all ready starting to plan the arrangements in his head.

"Can we also set up living quarters in the building?" I asked.

"But of course," Erik smiled. "Let me show you the top floor where former offices can be converted to living spaces for at least six people. I believe there is also a shower there."

After more exploration we judged the site suitable, better than I had anticipated, and Erik returned to his home while Blake and I made some plans. It was late in the afternoon when we remembered that Blake would have to return to pick up the other medics whom we had left in a café; by now they might be pretty drunk on the free wine that all the shopkeepers were offering their liberators. As Blake drove off I remembered I had not asked Erik about the Professor we were supposed to inquire about, so returned to the Gambetta house.

This time the maid showed me into the master's apartment immediately. She seemed a little unprofessionally friendly, I thought, but perhaps all French women reacted to men that way. Erik joined me in the library. This time his shirt was open almost all the way to the navel, showing even more of that silky black hair fanned over a well-developed chest and flat belly, all the way to the waistband.

"I'm sorry, I forgot to ask you a question. Are you familiar with a Professor von Osterhaus by any chance? I have been instructed to find him if possible."

Erik looked closely, perhaps anxiously, at me for an instant but then his face froze into its usual detached coolness. "I don't believe I have heard the name," he responded carefully.

So much for that, I thought. "By the way, is your name actually 'Erik'? I understood that was a code name."

He smiled briefly as if he had expected the question. "No, that is not my name, and I hope never to need to use it again. Now that you Americans are here, I can abandon it." He stopped, and I wondered if he intended to give me his real name or remain mysterious. After a moment he continued, "The family name is Westenburg, and I am Gerhard." He stood up formally and clicked his heels together as he offered his hand. I shook it but he did not release it immediately. Even his fingers felt silky to my rougher touch.

There was a small noise at the door. "Ah, come in, my dear," Gerhard said, releasing my hand promptly. I turned to greet one of the most beautiful women I had ever met. She was dark, slim, and graceful, with long black hair falling well below her shoulders. Her totally feminine hips emphasized her narrow waist. "May I introduce Sergeant — I'm afraid I did not ask your name."

"Bristow," I supplied. "Matt Bristow." I could not look away from her deep black eyes, accentuated skillfully with bluish makeup which matched her modish dress, and her lush, red lips just made for sex, I thought to myself.

"I am Lili," she purred, her deep voice tugging at my vitals. "May I call you 'Matt'?"

I am sure I blushed, not because of the question but because my mind was occupied with my picture of her spread out in bed, her full breasts heaving from my ministrations. "Of course," I stammered eventually.

She glided into the room and her fingertips trailed over Gerhard's shoulders as she passed behind him. She sank gracefully to a chair near us, the garden, visible through an

158

open door, her backdrop. The shadows had grown long there, the sun almost setting behind the house. I struggled to recover from her presence.

"You — you have a beautiful house," I croaked, returning to Gerhard with resolve to concentrate on my host for the moment. The only problem with that was that he was just as desirable in his own supermasculine way.

"Ah, merci, Sergeant — Matt," he smiled as if to suggest he had taken liberties with my name. "My parents bought this building years ago when we moved here from Austria. Each floor has two apartments, but this is the largest. Now there are just — we two — or is it, 'us two,' I am never sure in English." He glanced quickly at Lili; she did not offer help with the language but there was a spark between them, it seemed. "There are eight apartments, two on each floor, and of course there is the usual *chambre de bonne* on the fifth floor for the maid for each apartment."

It was a far cry from a Napa Valley vineyard. "You are Austrian?"

"Yes — does that surprise you?"

I was flustered. "Well, I guess I didn't expect — I mean I assumed you were French — "

"Nein — no. True natives recognize our accent, but it may not be noticeable to you. You see — " he moved nervously in his chair, the first time I had detected any sign that he was uncomfortable about something — "There were Jews among the ancestors, and we were not welcome — "

At that moment the maid entered silently and began to arrange dishes on the gleaming table in the center of the room. "You will stay for a simple cold supper with us, won't you — Matt?" Lili smoothly inserted herself in the conversation. Although I protested that I did not wish to intrude, they insisted. I caught the maid's eyes on me again, and

159

they seemed to imply more than simple curiosity. She seemed to switch her tail in my direction as she worked, but perhaps it was my imagination.

"A sherry apéritif?" Lili held a dainty glass nearly full of amber liquid, and I took it uncertainly. The maid was lighting a few candles and the room was soon golden as night came on. Oh, well, Blake would know where I was if he needed me, I reasoned. I hoped the other guys weren't too drunk when he found them.

The "simple supper" was not large but it was filling. Cold meats and a salad with the most delicious dressing I could remember tasting. First they served a white wine to accompany a slice of salmon in aspic and later red wine with spicy sausage slices, none of which I was familiar with. Evidently Paris was not starving, or at least not the Westenburgs. There was much touching between them, I noticed, during the meal. Their fingers would touch first, intimately, when passing dishes to each other. It would seem they were a particularly sensuous couple.

My wine glass was refilled whenever I set it down on the table. I found myself talking about my home and our vineyards as if we were old friends, which I suppose was a sign of feeling comfortable with gracious hosts. When I realized that I needed to use the toilet and stood up, I felt dizzy but truly refreshed for the first time since arriving in Europe. I started weaving down the hall where they directed me, but I guess I became confused. I started to open a door, but Lili, who I didn't realize was behind me, stopped me quickly and pointed to the next door.

"Oh, sorry – I guess I'm – a little drunk," I mumbled. She smiled carefully and watched me until I entered the toilet and closed the door. When I emerged she stood in front of the closed door with a smile on her face.

The maid had cleared the dishes and I realized that it was late. Gerhard was still sipping his brandy. He went to stand behind Lili's chair with his hand down the front of her dress, evidently caressing her breast but looking at me. Obviously he was thinking about having sex, a most attractive prospect indeed, and I realized I should leave. Before I could summon the words, Lili broke the somewhat awkward silence.

"Gerhard, what about apartment 2B for the Sergeant? I am sure the former tenants will never return. They fled to Spain, I believe."

"Ah, yes, my dear," Gerhard responded, "Why not? I am sure you will find almost everything you require upstairs, and it will certainly be more comfortable than some temporary arrangements you could make in the old garage. And perhaps a brandy before you go? Yes?"

Their faces swam before my eyes, and a sip of the heady brandy was enough to make my decision. "Well, I suppose if it is vacant — "

"Yes, yes — Claudine! Claudine will show you the way. Please be our guest."

"Oui — come," the maid gave a little curtsy, and I followed her, stumbling a little, after saying good night to my hosts. She climbed one flight and opened a door that appeared just like the door to the Westenburg apartment, but when I looked around inside the dusty furniture was not as luxurious. There was a bed made up with sheets and a thick comforter which looked very inviting, but Claudine took my hand. I looked at her, confused, but she pulled me into the hall again. "Come — *chambre de bonne*," she murmured. I had no idea what she was saying.

She led me to the top floor and into what was obviously her quarters — a small room with a narrow bed, a table, and a small closet. Without a word she lay on the bed and held up her arms to me. She had to help me to remove my clothes, but my memories of details are very cloudy.

161

19

In the morning I awoke soon after dawn with the rustlings of Claudine delivering a large croissant with jam and strong coffee to me in bed, after which she disappeared without a word, returning to work downstairs.

There was a stack of towels waiting for me in the rustic bathroom in 2B, but after bathing in the somewhat rusty water I went directly to the newly-selected clinic. I found the entire staff asleep on the floor of the top storey. Obviously they were suffering from hangovers, even Blake, but I could pretend to be virtuous and in command of the situation. They didn't ask where I had spent the night.

We worked hard that day to adapt the building to its new use. Our critical supplies were to be trucked in on the following day. In the meantime I reported to the command headquarters that we had begun work and gave them the new address. I was able to pick up accumulated cash payment for all of us in Charenton, the first pay we had received in weeks. There was another message waiting concerning the mysterious Professor von Osterhaus. In that regard, they passed on a message that had been received several weeks ago through some mysterious source: "East or west, a man's house is his castle." Whatever that was supposed to mean.

A Frenchman appeared at the new clinic, a distinguished gentleman in almost antique clothing, who introduced himself as a doctor (last name unpronounceable for me) and offering his general practice services. He spoke passable English, and I was happy to greet him. I had noticed him emerging from the Westenburg house just before he made his appearance, so I assumed that Gerhard had sent him. It was likely, I thought, that our military-based surgical

162

expertise would not be as much in demand as medical services in Paris, and I was right. The French hospital nearby would soon be back in operation, I was told, stocked with American supplies, of course. Until then we would serve the French public.

The cafés nearby were happy to serve us food but we had to use our own cash to pay for it. The command office said they would set up accounts to avoid this, but it would take time.

When I returned to the Westenburg house that evening, I found Gerhard working in the garden. Although the sun was all ready low, the day was hot and humid and he had stripped to a pair of loose shorts. His position, bending over to dig in the dirt around the untrimmed bushes, brought his superb derrière (I found myself thinking in the few French terms I knew) to prominence. His long legs were as muscular and hairy as his chest, and brought several fantasies to mind.

When he saw me he smiled and straightened up, and I was again mesmerized by his intense dark eyes and sensuous lips. Sweat dripped from the black silk of his chest and seeped into his waistband. I tried to avoid speculating of the part of his body hidden by those offending shorts.

"A new beginning," he commented. "It is time now to return to ordinary things, like gardening."

I nodded, finding it difficult to concentrate on his words, but he continued. "Would you join us at supper tonight?"

I shook my head, informing him that I had eaten with the others at a nearby restaurant. His look of disappointment was more than I would expect from an ordinary host. I excused myself, going to "my" apartment. I noticed the door was unlocked and there was no key in evidence. Apparently locking apartment doors was not expected – or was this a special case? At least it facilitated Claudine's joining me in the large, comfortable bed, waking me after

163

I had fallen asleep early and finishing the evening enjoyably. We could not really converse, but body language is entirely adequate during sex as I had discovered with Daisy in the mountain-top cabin.

When I returned to the house the next evening, the door to the Westenburg's apartment was standing open, and Gerhard hailed me as I started to climb the stairs. "At least join us for a little brandy," he suggested, and I could not refuse. This time I began sipping it slowly, feeling its heat immediately.

Lili was wearing tight slacks of a deep green which again she matched with her makeup. Her blouse was loose but her breasts filled it undeniably; the neck was open enough to show the upper curvatures. Gerhard's legs were enclosed in the usual black, clinging material, and as long as I ignored the alluring bulge in the crotch, I was not uneasy.

For a few minutes we spoke about the clinic and the needs for medical services in the neighborhood.

"What led you to settle in Charenton?" I inquired of them.

"Ah, yes," Gerhard smiled. "Charenton is slightly famous since it is here that the Marquis de Sade wrote many of his best works about sex and pain. Are you familiar with our Donatien Alphonse François?"

"Only slightly," I answered. Both of them were watching me closely. That night we were sitting in the living room that I had not been in previously. A huge grand piano graced one end of the room near the double doors to the garden that admitted only a slight breeze. The furniture was also grand; light gray damask chairs with green and pink touches surrounded a low cocktail table, and there was a large green leather couch nearby. Again long white tapers were our only light source. My hosts' chairs were close together across the table from me.

164

"We also believe that pain can augment sex in sometimes unpredictable, almost imponderable ways," Lili explained. She changed position by crossing her legs seductively. Gerhard's left leg bore the long swelling that my eyes frequently returned to involuntarily. I could clearly see the ridge around the head through the thin trousers. I am sure they saw me glancing at it, but showed no reaction.

I cleared my throat. "You mean whipping, branding, things like that?"

"Yes," she answered, "but in much more subtle ways, also." One of her hands slipped into the neck of her blouse and another button came dislodged. "Pinching nipples, as an example."

I could feel my crotch tighten slightly. "Oh, of course," I nodded. "I had never thought of that as pain, however. Just — play?" I sounded more blasé than I felt.

"Of course," she responded, her hand still under her dress. I could see the fingers moving, and more of her other breast came into view as the blouse opened more. I took another sip of brandy.

"It is not necessary to use special equipment. Teeth can be an excellent source of pain," Gerhard inserted. "Nibbling the clitoris, for example, or — perhaps best of all is the tender skin just under the head of the penis." I could see his own organ growing in length as he spoke, a growth that I also experienced.

Lili's hand came to rest on his thigh, at first casually but then gripping it tightly, but her eyes never left mine.

"What if — the other person — doesn't really want — I mean, if it disturbs instead of enhancing — " I wasn't really sure what I meant.

Lili shrugged. "I suppose there are such people. I believe they would not be very good lovers." She looked directly at Gerhard, and then moved her hand to caress the side of his face. This time he was unreactive, his attention focused on me.

"Having something large pushed up your rectum, for instance," he said blandly, "might be excruciatingly painful as well as deliciously pleasureful."

It was a horrifying thought, and yet I intuitively knew that he was right under certain conditions. Pain, and the fear of pain which was sometimes more powerful, set my mind racing and my senses to maximal peaks of sensitivity. Fear was a dominating force when battle was raging all around us, and yet that fear also sharpened our edges and stirred our hormones.

Of course the mass throbbing in Gerhard's crotch was the unidentified intruder he was suggesting. At the moment, for me the pleasure associated with that picture dwarfed the discomfort that might accompany it, and I stiffened appreciably.

Lili sounded annoyed. "Why are men always so concerned about their asses?" Somehow from her lips the word seemed terribly obscene.

"In some cultures being penetrated is the ultimate shame for a man," Gerhard explained patiently, glancing at her, bemused. "Don't you agree, Matt?" Returning his attention to me, his erection grew quickly, and they both knew it had my full attention. That seemed to irritate Lili.

"Breasts are so much more sensitive," she murmured, unbuttoning her blouse to expose her magnificent pair, breasts that I had dreamed about repeatedly since meeting her only days ago. Firm and round, crested with pinkish-brown nipples that already seemed tense, they cried out for adoration. My erection grew quickly down my leg, and both pairs of eyes observed it closely. The action had shifted to her court, at least for the moment.

"We know you have beautiful breasts, my dear," Gerhard murmured to her. He took the closest nipple between his fingers, and I saw his nails bite into her flesh. Their patrician faces remained bland, but I could see more fire spring up in her eyes.

Abruptly Gerhard broke off the contact and stood up. "More brandy?" he asked smoothly, bringing the bottle over to me. His erection was even more prominent when he stood, but he was obviously showing it off — for me or for Lili? My mouth was dry, and I had unconsciously been sipping the brandy as if it were water. Gerhard refilled my glass and his; he ignored Lili's, which was still half full. This time he turned to place the bottle on the piano, taking several moments to complete the simple action, and bringing his luscious butt into view. I sipped my brandy as my eyes devoured it openly. He looked over his shoulder at me, and after assuring himself of my reaction he returned to his chair with a tiny smile.

"Bondage may be the route to a deeper understanding of one's self," Gerhard said quietly, almost ominously. He could see uncertainty in my face; he probably could also see the fascination being produced. "To be immobilized, even if it is frightening at first, can in the end be enlightenment to the uninitiated. For instance, if I were to tie you up to the wall and apply the whip, you might scream but at the same time experience the most supreme of orgasms."

His cock actually lurched stiffly at the thought, tenting the trousers massively. I knew he could see mine struggling to escape from its bonds; his eyes, penetrating and uncompromising, were fixed on my crotch without any sign of embarrassment or attempt at concealment.

There was no doubt in my mind that being on either the active or passive side of that equation could be an exquisite sexual experience for Gerhard and me, although my mind

167

summarily discarded the role with Lili. I could not envision either whipping Lili or being whipped by her. For me that picture was restricted to other men.

Lili's eyes moved to the same spots, both crotches coming in for intense scrutiny, which was in itself electrifying. Watching them throbbing, she gave a little moan and her legs spread widely. She slumped down a little in her chair, and I could see a spot in the crotch of her slacks grow damp. The tense silence in the room was profound. The very act of avoiding the action we were contemplating was increasing the tension to the extreme.

"I think the imposition of pain can also be much more subtle," I said after a moment, supersensitive to the currents in the room. "Withholding of a prize or reward can also constitute pain, can't it?"

Gerhard looked at me closely. "Deprivation is, of course, one type of punishment. It was probably one of the elements that informed Sade's writing during his imprisonment." He looked at me more intently, and I thought I detected some suspicion in his expression.

I knew it was necessary for me to leave, to leave before being devoured or being destroyed by denial of that end. I rose in preparation for departure, but of course their eyes feasted on my obvious arousal. "It is late and I must get some rest," I ventured. "Can we resume our discussion later?"

At that moment I was in control, and I think I saw a hint of respect in Gerhard's eyes. Lili was more than crestfallen — her blatant sexuality had been refused. They followed me into the hall, but as I walked toward the door I heard a thump somewhere behind me. It was not a sound they had made — perhaps from the floor above? I thought that apartment was empty. Lili remained behind as Gerhard escorted me to the door and, as I turned to say my farewell,

I saw her enter the room across the hall as she rebuttoned her blouse.

I went to bed but could not quiet my appetites whetted so expertly by my hosts. I was both the hunter and the hunted; the farm boy from the Napa Valley in the snares of the wealthy, European intellectuals with backgrounds of centuries of decadence that brought its own lures. I was out of my element, but could not deny the intense physical stimulation of the visions they produced. I instinctively realized that both feeling pain and giving pain could be sexual experiences at a mystical, spiritual level. I masturbated forcefully and repeatedly, my fantasies wild and confused, vacillating between them with myself on top and on the bottom, until I was exhausted and finally slept.

At least the Westenburgs managed to displace the memories of Dr. Mills, grief which frequently came flooding back to me in those minutes just before sleep erases the world.

I did not see the Westenburgs for a few days, but I saw the doctor coming and going almost every day. Could he have been one of their previous underground members? When he visited the Clinic he seemed quite outdated in regard to current drugs; for instance he was unfamiliar with penicillin, which was in standard practice with us although sometimes difficult to obtain. Of course he had been out of touch with medical advances for about four years, so that was understandable. His medical knowledge was as outmoded as his waxed mustache and his bowler hat.

Once or twice during the next few days I climbed the stairs to the little *chambre* to which Claudine had taken me. She always seemed happy to see me, but I have no idea of her real thoughts. We made each other happy for those moments, at least. My fantasies involved the Westenburgs in their marital bed.

I avoided the mysterious Austrians for another reason

— I needed to explore in my own mind how I felt about some of their ideas, and I was also trying to determine what it was that was nagging at my brain, something unexplained by what they had told me. And in another compartment of my brain were the dispatches from headquarters about the missing Professor. A second message with the code, "East or west, a man's house is his castle" was passed on. What the hell could be the significance of an ordinary cliché like that?

When I next encountered Gerhard, I couldn't resist his suggestion. When I entered the house he was standing at his door, waiting for me just inside the entrance. He wore only a black leather jockstrap, and his body was as sleek and enticing as I had dreamed. The leather almost seemed a part of his body, the long, silky black body hair serving to focus my eyes on the black bulge in his crotch.

"I would like to show you something," he intoned. "Something that I think will please you."

He led the way to the cavernous living room; we passed the door to the forbidden room, but it was closed. Lili, totally nude, was kneeling in the place where the low table had been on my previous visit. Her wrists were bound together with leather straps and her eyes were shadowed, downcast in slavish submission. Her long hair hung down nearly to the floor, draping her face in glossy cascades, and more was visible between her legs near the floor. Her hips flared as the classical framing of her sex.

Gerhard motioned me to the damask chair opposite her. Gerhard took a chair behind Lili, his arms hanging loosely at his sides, and watched my face. A globular glass of brandy waited at my elbow, and for a few moments I sipped the heady brew in the complete silence of the night. His eyes were intense and his breathing seemed rapid, his swelling pectorals with their fans of black strands broadening with each intake. Lili seemed calm and quiet, but I could not see the expression on her face.

"Come here, Lili," I finally commanded, and without raising her head she moved forward on her knees without hesitation. I unbuckled my belt and opened my fly, but stopped there. "What do you want, Lili?" I asked in a low voice. For the first time she looked up at me, and the pleading in her eyes was palpable. There was no need for an answer. I rose briefly and lowered my pants to the floor, my erection springing upward in relief, and then regained my seat. Both sets of eyes were fixed on the object of their desire. The bulge in Gerhard's jockstrap was enlarging.

Slowly Lili reached out and grasped me with both hands that were still lashed together; she caressed me, first upward and then back, bringing a clear drop of moisture to the tip. My jaws clenched with the pressure, denying myself the immediate gratification she could have produced. Her smooth hands roved over the head and shaft expertly; the pressure became nearly unbearable.

She almost purred her approval. "Sehr schön, so schön."

"Sit on it, Lili," I ordered. Her hands froze for a moment, her grip almost painful, and then she rose and did as she had been commanded. The black-etched skin-framed sheath, all ready moist and receptive, closed over me like a tight glove. Even as she engulfed me she spasmed and moaned, throwing her head back and thrusting her breasts forward to my waiting lips.

Over her shoulder I saw Gerhard slump down in his chair, his jock strap straining upward. His eyes were fixed on our coupling like a vulture eying his prey, but it was difficult to discern which of us was the primary focus. And in turn he was an active player in the drama Lili and I were acting out in his audience. I knew how to bridge this fantasy gap.

With my hands under Lili's buttocks, I rose and, still lodged deeply in her innermost recesses, walked with her,

171

legs wrapped around my waist, to Gerhard. I gently deposited her in Gerhard's lap as I crouched to begin my fucking movements. His eyes widened, her weight painful on his covered erection, as I had assumed. Our eyes met and held as I set up a rhythm. Control was the issue between us. It was easy to conceive that my action was meant for him as well. I was only inches away from filling his rectum as he had challenged me. His previously stoic countenance slowly transformed to an anguished grimace, as if he could feel me entering him forcefully.

His hands were busy in his lap for a moment and then I felt his entrance between her buttocks. Inward he moved, and Lili cried out in pain and pleasure. His rigidity matched mine, pressing against me through the thin tissue between us, as I moved in and out. Our gazes remained locked together, our contact intrinsic with Lili our intermediary. My teeth fastened again on her tense nipples.

I moved for both of us, sliding over him repeatedly, forcing him to react to me. His eyes glazed and then closed, but his arms hung down limply as if to emphasize his passivity at the moment. I could feel his prominent ridge as mine moved over it, pressing firmly. Lili moaned and thrashed erratically, increasing the pleasurable contact for all of us. Her fettered fingers strummed her clitoris wildly. I increased the pace and he stiffened even more; I knew I was nearing climax, but struggled to wait until I detected the signs in his agitated face.

At the last moment I withdrew and pressed against Lili's belly, streaking her whitely, explosively. Gerhard strained forward to watch over Lili's shoulder, and with my first spurt he groaned and thrust upward, our climaxes simultaneous. Lili screamed, the recipient of our passions inside and out. I clasped her face to mine, thrusting my tongue between her teeth and muffling her cries. My brain whirled but my gaze remained fixed on Gerhard's face, contorted almost unrecognizably.

Several moments passed before we had sufficiently recovered to break the connection. When I released her, Lili sagged to the floor in exhaustion. Gerhard sat stunned, still dripping on the thick carpet, his eyes following my movements. After a moment I retrieved my clothing, dressing slowly, and still they remained immobile. Deliberately I stood in full uniform, the rough khaki contrasting with their subdued damask and silk, looking down at them as I slowly finished my brandy. Then I quietly left and returned to my apartment above.

I was still struggling to understand my reactions to the evening's tableau. Where did aggression end and sadism begin? Was unlimited control more or less satisfying than receptivity? I believed I would discover more about myself before that night ended. I was confident that I knew what the next steps would be.

I stretched out on my belly on the bed nude, my face cradled in my arms on the pillow, and waited. Time passed but I was still very alert when I heard the apartment door open and footsteps approaching the bedroom. There was no attempt at stealth; I heard every movement. I lay still as if sleeping. We both knew I was awake. The unseen figure apparently stood looking down at me for a moment and then I felt the added weight to the bed. First a finger entered me, but then almost immediately his entire thick member penetrated in one prolonged push, extending deeper than I had ever remembered feeling before. I resisted the impulse to cry out – I had steeled myself for it.

He set up a punishing rhythm as if determined to elicit a response, any response, but I remained mute. He held me down by my shoulders, imprisoning me. It was not necessary. I could not completely control my involuntary reciprocal movements, however; I shoved upward to meet his thrusts, hungry for all he could give, all this in complete silence. Finally it was he who broke the spell, howling his release into my ear as he lurched to the depths.

As he lay gasping, stretched out over me, I could feel his sweat puddling on my back, and could picture the silken hair soaked and matted on his chest and belly. I could feel each strand imparting its magical touch to my thirsty skin, and I was content. After a few moments he rose and his footsteps returned down the hall. I heard the apartment door close. Now I would sleep with a smile on my face, enjoying the sticky dampness I had deposited on the sheet under me during Gerhard's visit.

I t was Sunday morning but I was uneasy and couldn't sleep. I dressed and went to the staff rooms at the Clinic, hoping to find an early riser, someone to have breakfast with.

I opened the first door quietly but the two occupants, hard-working medics whom I knew only casually, were still asleep — in fact they were asleep in one bed, their arms wrapped around each other. I smiled, knowing that I must remember not to reveal my knowledge of their relationship. The next door was Blake's, I discovered; when I peered in he sat up quickly, nude above the sheet, and sleepily invited me in.

"Sorry to wake you," I whispered, and shut the door quietly behind me. "I was just looking for a breakfast companion."

"Oh, sure," he grinned, but didn't leave the bed. After a moment more of hesitation, I intuited that he had a morning hardon and didn't want me to see him that way. Deliberately I turned to survey his room, which he had decorated himself, to give him opportunity to cover his embarrassment. I was right; as soon as I turned away he sprang out of bed and hurriedly pulled on his shorts.

The rooms were quite adequate, the way they had been constructed and decorated, I thought. The temporary walls didn't extend to the ceiling, of course, and I smiled at the thought of the noises that must issue from the coupling next door. The paint was fresh, and Blake had mounted enlargements of pictures taken during the liberation celebration and more recently during the Clinic construction.

175

The largest picture showed Blake and me in our jeep, and several others included me prominently. I was somewhat embarrassed by his concentration on me in his collection.

"You've made quite a collection here," I smiled at him as he pulled on his pants, a sizable bulge still prominent. "I thought Rita Hayworth pin-ups were the standard decoration these days. . .?"

"To each his own," Blake answered casually. "A man's home is his castle, they say."

I stared at him for a moment, my thoughts tumbling. I struck my forehead with my fist. "Of course! Home! That's what was wrong!"

"Huh?" Blake was confused.

"Forget breakfast. Come with me. We've got a job to do."

Blake still had no idea what I was thinking when I knocked on Gerhard's door a few minutes later. He opened the door and looked curiously at us, blocking the door, but I eased him aside and entered without ceremony, bringing Blake with me. "I'm sorry to intrude, Gerhard, but we are on official business. Come, Blake."

I walked resolutely down the hall and opened the door that I had been forbidden to enter. Gerhard shouted, "No!" but I entered the small room, Blake at my heels. The window was shuttered and the air was stale, but in the room was a small bed occupied by someone whom I could not identify, and by the bed was the French doctor, obviously in the process of ministering to his patient. Lili stood on the other side of the bed, her eyes wide and staring at our intrusion.

The man on the bed was old and frail. His hair was white and seemed unkempt and his thin arms and delicate hands were limp above the sheet. Most remarkable was his face, lined and pale, but distorted on one side – drawn back in a contortion that could only have one explanation. His pale eyes found me with some difficulty.

"Good morning, Doctor," I muttered. "You seem to have a seriously ill patient here. I assume this is Professor von Osterhaus?"

Lili gasped and the doctor stared at me in confusion. Gerhard moved to stand beside Lili, his arm around her shoulder. No one answered my question except by their silence.

"What is the patient's condition, Doctor?" I asked. Blake stirred himself to move to the bedside and check the patient's pulse. The doctor stammered, lapsing into French.

"I believe he has had a stroke, is that not so?" I interrupted him pointedly. "Is he currently paralyzed?"

The doctor nodded. "Oui, his left side − " he shrugged, ". . . very weak − cannot stand or speak properly." I nodded.

"Is he in any immediate danger?" I insisted.

Again he shrugged; it was apparently a favorite French gesture, but it could mean anything. "No, I − no, but − it is difficult to care for him here."

I nodded. "Of course." I turned to Gerhard. "We have been asked to locate the Professor − your father, no?" Gerhard remained silent, his lips tight. "Or is he your father, Lili? Have you been caring for your father-in-law?"

Lili looked stricken but remained silent; Gerhard finally answered, his face set and hostile. "Lili is my sister, not my wife, and this man is indeed our father."

Several loose ends became tied with that statement, but it would take some time before I could digest all the implications.

"I must report the situation to Washington. In the meantime, I'm afraid I must place you and Lili under house

177

arrest, at least until I get clearance from Washington."

Blake had continued to perform a cursory examination as we spoke. After we left the apartment, I asked him what he had found.

"A profound weakness on the left — apparently a cerebrovascular accident to the right hemisphere, either from a clot or bleeding," he responded professionally. "Some reflexes are hyperactive."

He looked at me strangely. "How did you know what you would find?" he asked curiously as we climbed into the jeep for a quick trip to command headquarters.

"You know about that strange code phrase the Pentagon reported about the mysterious professor? 'East or west, a man's house is his castle?' Until you gave the correct phraseology this morning, I couldn't figure out what was wrong with it. Also, in German, 'Osterhaus' can be translated 'eastern house,' and the name they are using, 'Westenburg,' can be translated 'western castle.' But the correct phrase is 'a man's *home* is his castle,' and that was the important clue. When you said it, it clicked into place." I didn't want to mention how I came to my suspicions about the special room where the professor lay, and he didn't ask.

When I reported our findings to headquarters there was some excitement in sending the message. The next day we received the response from official Washington. According to the Pentagon, the Austrian professor had once been an important contact for information and research on some big government "project" — that word again, an unusual word in Army terminology. Now that we had learned that he was incapacitated, there would be no more inquiries.

At the end of the message, there was an unusual postscript: "Well done, Napa-noodle."

I will not relate the details of the next months of blood and savagery spent in the Ardennes, later called the Battle of the Bulge. The winter was severe and both the allied and German armies were ravaged and driven to sub-human behavior by their determination to rule Europe. Frostbite was rampant on both sides because of lack of proper footwear. The wounded were sometimes left behind to freeze when retreat was required. It would be years before some of the bodies were recovered. We saw the lucky ones, those who could be treated; some committed suicide rather than face the impossible horror of that war.

There was difficulty in keeping our patients warm, as well as ourselves. Blake and I frequently slept together, fully clothed and wrapped in blankets, to keep warm. Sex was not on our minds, or at least not on mine. My usual optimistic approach to life took a beating that winter. I told myself that perhaps it was fortunate, in a way, that Dr. Mills had not lived to experience the profound disintegration of civilization that had become so apparent. I still missed him acutely.

Our unit had left our "vacation" in Paris about the time that the German V-2 rockets began to fall there. The British took Brussels and Antwerp, and the Americans breached the Siegfried Line to take Aachen. French armored forces took Strasbourg in Alsace. We were holed up in Bastogne until Gen. Patton and his tanks broke through on the day after Christmas, and then we pursued the enemy to the Rhine River where we became bogged down. The Russian forces that survived Stalingrad took Budapest and, by April, Vienna, while we were finally able to break through at

Remagen. The allied forces in Italy took Bologna and pushed north. Eventually most of the enemy forces surrendered, but Amsterdam and much of The Netherlands remained pockets of largely passive resistance. We were transferred there in the spring.

In the meantime the cruelty of man was becoming more and more obvious. The bombing of German targets had increased resulting in monstrous casualties, and Tokyo was also being bombed with devastating results. The allied leaders had met in Yalta, but there was much grumbling about the deals made there by both sides. There was general mourning in April when President Roosevelt died; I wondered how my father felt about that, since he had previously not been a supporter of his social programs. Perhaps the new President Truman would be more to his liking.

Blake and I were both wounded, neither seriously, several times during those winter months. By April we were the only remaining members of our original unit to survive. There was no real battle to liberate Amsterdam because the enemy was so disheartened by their other defeats, but the city was almost deathly quiet. When we entered the city we found the people subdued but not really terrorized. Only the Jews had been persecuted there, most of them shipped away on trains with concealed destinations and never seen again. Those who remained had nearly starved, living in cramped hiding places. The last year had been the worst for the residents of the city, because food had become scarce for everyone in German-occupied territories. Now the people ventured into the streets hesitantly, having had little communication with the outside world for years. It was a far cry from our triumphant entry into Paris only eight months earlier.

Some of the Jews who remained in the city had been concealed for years in little houses or lofts attached to larger mansions on the canals; we learned about these hiding places from patients who made an appearance at the clinic in the following weeks. An *achterhuis*, literally an "outhouse," was intended for a son and his wife, or a retired parent, to occupy temporarily when the family was expanding.

We were ordered to set up our operations in a brick building that had been a school at one time. When the Germans had occupied the city they had used the building for their command headquarters. We were warned that some of the enemy might still be hiding in the remnants of the city, either too frightened to surrender to the Americans or determined to die in last ditch efforts on behalf of the Heimat. We no longer hesitated to wear pistols as we went about our duties.

It appeared that the enemy had left the building with little preparation, since there were German papers and paraphernalia scattered everywhere. It had apparently been headquarters for the Germanische SS, the political military, and the *Sicherheits Dienst* (Security Service), but there were also pieces of correspondence bearing the letterhead of the *Geheime Staatspolizei* which I figured was the full name of the Gestapo. Parts of black SS uniforms were left draped over chairs, and even portions of dried food left behind on desks by officers caught unaware of their plight until the last minute.

It was relatively easy to identify the office of the chief officer, since it was the most elaborately furnished. In the drawer of a massively ornate desk were keys labeled carefully for the other rooms used for various purposes. It was obvious that we would have to secure the building before we could begin our task of setting up a clinic for the pitiable denizens of the city who were beginning to emerge cautiously from hiding.

I set the men to explore the building, guns at the ready,

with the keys found in the desk, starting at the front door and working upward. Soon all the doors on each floor were standing open and none of the enemy had been encountered.

"Here's one that looks different — like a house key," Blake remarked, fingering the large ring of assorted keys. "It's labelled 'Albrecht Dürerstraat,' which is a street name I noticed just a block away. And here's a number, '58.' Perhaps where the chief of the SS lived?"

I shrugged. "We can check it out, when we get this building secured. How about the basement?" I asked. Two of the men descended the stairs as I returned to the office, but soon there was a shout and I ran down the stairs, treads worn in shallow depressions by thousands of children's scuffling feet over the years, to the room the men indicated. The door was locked and none of the keys fitted, they said, but they thought they heard sounds inside.

I returned to the office and searched the drawers again. In the back of a small drawer, hanging on a nail, was a single key that apparently had received special attention. When fitted into the lock the latch responded, but the next question was what we could expect inside. I drew my pistol, as did the others, and cautiously entered the silent darkness with a flashlight.

In the intense-black subterranean room were hooks and chains hanging from the beams overhead, rings mounted on the thick walls, and a low, rough-sawn table. It appeared to be a room fitted for torture of prisoners as in medieval times. The floor and walls were stained dark in places, which was probably from blood. On the table was the emaciated figure of a naked man strapped down to the rough surface. He appeared to be dead until I looked more closely and noticed slight movements of his chest.

We approached cautiously, not knowing what to expect.

His eyes were closed, but when I shone my light into his face they opened slightly. He was alive, but barely.

Quickly we released his bonds but he did not react, remaining as if frozen in place. I ordered the men with me to bring a stretcher and drinking water, and they dashed up the stairs to unpack the supplies needed from trucks outside. I remained with the victim.

I leaned over him and shone the light on my face so he could see me better. His eyes seemed glazed and at first I thought he might have been blinded. His cheeks were covered with a rough, brown beard that seemed to be several weeks old. I began to talk to him softly, soothingly, forgetting that he probably did not understand my language in any case. His eyes, a beautiful blue-green, slowly seemed to regain some recognition of his surroundings. I began to stroke his forehead. At my first touch he jerked as if expecting a blow, but then, perhaps from the combination of my soothing voice and calming touch, I saw tears form at the corners of his eyes. It was the first indication that he was able to feel a human emotion. Without thinking I bent and kissed his slack lips gently. When I looked back he was staring at me intently – but then the crew arrived with the stretcher and moved him to it.

"Be gentle with him!" The men looked at me a little strangely. After their experiences in the aid station and the rush of battle, they had forgotten the art of handling fragile patients who were not actually bleeding.

"Where should we take him?"

Where indeed? Nothing had been set up yet for caring for patients. Then I remembered the key that Blake had mentioned. I motioned them to bring him to the office where we gave him some water to drink.

In better light the torture he had undergone became apparent. He was truly emaciated, and old welts were visible on his chest, legs, and back. It looked like he had been whipped repeatedly, probably during questioning or because of some infractions of commands. There were small burns on his chest and belly and even on his penis, almost certainly from cigarette butts. All his body hair had been shaven away. His head had not been shaven but the hair shorn to less than an inch long.

Blake gave me the key he had spotted and he and I set off to find the address. As he remembered, it was only about a block away. On one side of the street were large apartment houses, three or four storeys high, with smaller houses with untrimmed hedges on the other side. The key operated the lock in the house numbered 58, which was one of the larger buildings, and we entered cautiously, guns drawn.

The first floor apartment was rather grand, with heavy, upholstered furniture and oriental rugs on the floors. Again there was evidence of a hasty departure, with some food still in the ancient ice box in the small kitchen. Someone had dusted fairly recently. In the large bedroom closet were full black and silver uniforms of a high-ranking SS officer, hanging neatly as if ready for a servant to dress his master. There was also a huge bed with feather-down comforters and thick pillows. The officer had lived well, it seemed.

"Bring him here," I directed Blake. "I can live here and care for him until we have a better place set up." I could tell that Blake was uncertain about the wisdom of that idea, and I realized that I didn't totally understand the decision myself. He did not question me, but returned to the old school house while I explored the building further.

The apartments above number 58 seemed empty, and no one answered my calls. All the doors were locked, and the key marked "58" did not fit them. They would have to be checked out, of course. I learned later that the neighborhood that been largely Jewish, and most of the people had been sent away by the Germans.

184

By this time the men had arrived with the stretcher, and we carefully moved the victim to the huge, soft bed. I brought him some stale bread and cooked sausage I found in the kitchen, hoping it was not spoiled.

He only nibbled on the food at first, and I helped him drink more water between his tiny bites. Dehydration was a major problem, I knew. I could see the men watching me questioningly, never having seen me in that caring role before. Even I didn't understand why this young man was so important to me. Finally I instructed one of the men to stay with him, to help him to eat and drink as he was able, and the rest of us returned to our primary task.

It was after dark when I was able to return to the apartment. The medic reported that he had bathed his wounds and found nothing of a major medical problem. The young man had gone to sleep soon after we had left, and had not stirred. I had brought more food, but that could wait. His breathing seemed normal and I relieved the medic; I would be there when he awoke if he needed more attention. I found that there was actually hot water in the bathroom, probably from a heater in the basement, and I took my first real bath in weeks. The patient had not moved when I returned. I moved one of the feather comforters to the floor for my bed and went to sleep, my ear tuned for any sounds.

That was the first of several nights I spent on the floor of the officer's bedroom. Whenever the young man was awake I urged him to eat and drink, and gradually he began to respond, first struggling to sit up with my help, and soon he was able to walk stiffly and with assistance to the bathroom which was part of the bedroom suite. He seemed to understand what I said to him, or perhaps it was the tone of my voice that he responded to. He remained mute. I asked for volunteers among the men to help me care for him, and it became a matter of pride for them to assist me

185

nurse him back to health. He became a symbol of the horror of the war that controlled our every act.

On the fourth night, I was smoothing a so-called healing salve on his welts; I wasn't convinced it would do much good but might reduce the amount of scarring somewhat. I noticed that there were small, stubbly hairs beginning to show up, especially in his groin. He would have a regrowth soon. As usual I was talking to him, not saying much of note because I did not expect him to understand, when I heard him make a rasping noise in his throat. At first I thought he was choking, but then he spoke hoarsely, "Are you American?"

My jaw dropped; he was talking, and in English!

"Yes, yes!" I answered. "You speak English?"

Again he cleared his throat before he responded. "Not good – well. . . "

"Any is much better than none," I smiled. "We were afraid you might never speak, because of – what you must have gone through. . . "

He turned his head away for a moment, but then swung back to me. "The Germans?"

"Gone. Most have surrendered. The war is almost over."

He lay looking at the ceiling for several minutes, silent. I could almost see the stages of relaxation taking place in his face at the news. His unusually large blue-green eyes were now clear and had lost the startled look there earlier. He went back to sleep, but when I returned a couple of hours later to make my bed on the floor, he awoke.

"Would you like me to shave your face?" I asked. He looked at me for a moment; I don't think he realized until then that he had grown a ragged beard. He nodded but I saw fright in his eyes when he first saw the blade in my hand. I smoothed on some of my soap, working it into the beard, and gently shaved him clean. I was struck by the fine lines of his face, the masculine jaw, and especially the lush lips that almost begged to be kissed. So I kissed him, smiling to show that I approved of his fresh appearance. There were still questions in his eyes, but he did not flinch.

When I started to arrange my bed on the floor, he spoke again. "Sleep here, in bed, beside me." He patted the soft surface of the wide bed invitingly; I crawled in beside him and surrendered to the luxury of feather comforts. During the night I awoke to find his bony arm flung over my chest. I smiled and turned to wrap it a little tighter around me, nuzzling my back against him, and slept content.

The next evening when I returned to the apartment, he met me at the door, wearing one of my old fatigue uniforms. The medic who had been with him that day beamed.

"He says he doesn't need to be babied anymore, or at least I think that's what he said. His English is not too good, but at least he's talking. And he's developing an appetite like a horse!"

"He's got a lot to make up for," I grinned, clapping him on the shoulder that was still mostly bone and sinew.

He usually tired quickly, but remained awake all that evening. When he seemed comfortable I asked him his name. I could not understand at first what he said; the sound seemed to start with a "H" or was it a "G" or − ? When he saw my confusion, he said, "You may not be able to make some of our sounds. My name is also common in France, where it is pronounced 'Gerard.'"

"OK, Gerard, that's a major step forward. Can you tell me more about yourself? Not anything that's distressing, just − whatever you want to tell me."

He said he was twenty-three years old, was Dutch by birth but had married a French girl and had lived in France for several years, working in his father-in-law's apple

187

orchard. His mother was Jewish and so he went into hiding when the war started; since he lived in France he was not really considered Dutch but he was not legally permitted to live in France. He ran errands for the underground, including trips to Amsterdam and other spy cells in The Netherlands. He was in Amsterdam trying to protect his parents when the Wehrmacht invaded Normandy. He was told that his wife and her parents died while trying to defend their home from seizure. He continued to carry messages and helped to coordinate underground activities until about four months before we arrived, when he was captured and imprisoned in the building where we had found him.

Like most Dutch school children, he had been taught English in the classroom but rarely had the opportunity to practice conversational English. To understand some of his sentences took some multiple-choice questions from me to fill in the gaps, but our eyes and body language served well in times of confusion. That night when we went to bed together, it seemed only natural that we went to sleep with our arms around each other. He was so thin that it couldn't be called cuddling exactly, but he felt good to me.

After we had set up the Clinic and made it known that we were available for health care of the citizenry, we were overwhelmed by the needy patients. Many, especially the Jewish residents, had had no contact with medical practitioners during years of occupation, and relatively simple problems had become serious; for example, poor dental care had led to massive abscesses and systemic infections, which penicillin frequently improved promptly. One patient reported that, when he had needed a tooth filling, the dentist had been required to use a drill powered by a foot treadle because of the lack of electricity.

Some of the physicians assigned to us, usually surgeons experienced in trauma, were required to brush up on newer approaches to general medicine. It was an exciting time and a depressing time; we usually could make significant gains in health care but the underlying causes and the deprivation accompanying the illnesses were disheartening. However, the news from the war front was encouraging.

More and more I looked forward to my evenings with Gerard. Every day I could see improvement in both his physical and mental condition. Sometimes I sensed he became depressed but tried to conceal it from me. One night while applying an ointment to his fading welts, he sighed and I tried to explore his feelings.

"What's the matter? Tired?"

"No, not really," he responded.

I hesitated a moment but then blundered ahead. "Hungry again?" His voracious appetite, now that he was recovering well, was a frequent topic for jokes.

"No, no — it's just — I suppose the marks of the whip will always be there, won't they? I will never be able to show my body in public, I guess. . . ."

"Not at all," I assured him. "I doubt they will be more than barely visible soon. . . Perhaps the psychological marks will be more permanent than the physical ones."

He was quiet for several minutes while I continued to massage his back and then moved to his thighs striped with now-healing slashes. The depressions between his ribs were filling in nicely now that his nutrition was improved, and his butt was already alluring to me. Of course I had not mentioned that. I did not want to give the impression that I expected something from him in return for my protection, but I admitted to myself my increasing interest in him as a lovable man. Since he had been married before the war I had to assume he was heterosexual.

I rolled him over on his freshly-treated back and met with a towering hardon; as Dr. Mills would have said, that marked a point of progress from a medical point of view. I tried to ignore it for my own comfort, but my hands were shaking.

"I'm sorry," he breathed.

"About this?" I gripped his boner and shook it playfully for a moment. "No need to be sorry — in fact I envy you."

"You — envy me?" His cock swelled even more as I massaged his chest, and I noticed his nipples were tensing. They appeared to have been stretched or mangled by his tormentors.

"That beautiful foreskin," I chuckled. "I've always wished I had one." He did not respond, probably thinking it was a strange thing to say. That night I masturbated twice while bathing and before climbing into bed with him. Fortunately he was already asleep.

Now that he was greatly improved, he insisted on cooking dinner for me when I returned to the apartment in the evenings, although our food supply was spotty and sometimes boringly predictable. There had been a flourishing Black Market in the city during the war which remained our most dependable source of food. We had yet to speak of his experiences as a prisoner, and I did not introduce the subject.

Blake became a frequent visitor, almost like a friendly neighbor dropping in for coffee. He and Gerard became great friends in a short time, but Gerard's eyes always sought me out when trying to express an important thought. Frequently I found Blake's eyes on me with a similar expression, but decided he was a little envious of the comradeship Gerard and I felt together.

More and more our conversations took place in bed; it wasn't intended to lead to anything specific, but we frequently talked late into the night about our interests and desires, our lives to that point. Since both of us had backgrounds in farming and growing things, he in apple orchards and I in grape vineyards, it was natural to relate much of life's problems to nature's wisdom and order of things. We did not speak of sex specifically, but it seemed that we instinctively understood each other there as well. He began to make it a point to return my good night kiss, a habit I had maintained, and so I was not surprised one night to find us naturally moving from a good night kiss to gentle sexuality. We didn't talk about it, we just did it, which is the way it should happen, I thought.

I won't deny that his large, uncircumcised cock was a major attraction. As our relationship developed to include more varied sexual activities, I spent hours with that fascinating foreskin until he would clutch me in desperation, his orgasm demanding and forceful. He sometimes teased me, also, a favorite pastime being his tongue pressing and probing tantalizingly into my butt until I begged for something more. For the first time in my life I experienced a domestic relationship that was totally satisfying, coming home from work to a mate whom I loved and who seemed to love me, who shared my basic philosophy about life, and with whom sharing our bodies without reservation was natural and deeply satisfying.

He even took to kissing me goodbye at the front door when I left for duty at the Clinic each morning; I liked that. When I held him in my arms on the doorstep for the first time I realized that he was as tall as I and that, when we were able to put more meat on his bones, he would be a handsome man indeed. The hair on his head was growing back in tight, brown curls.

Mail from home finally caught up with me, floods of it, some originating several months previously. Little Paul was very active, into all kinds of minor trouble if left to his own devices, and that report brought a grin to my face. He was growing rapidly. Daisy had become his foster mother in

191

many respects, Martha reported. Perhaps Martha was a little old to appreciate his innocent mischief, whereas Daisy was of a better age to cope with it. Daisy had become very much a part of the family and her past trauma seemed firmly relegated to the past.

There was even a letter from Laura. Her first affair with the Berkeley student had peetered out after a few months, but she was intelligent enough to work through her understandable depression and be open to the future. She had befriended Daisy who showed some artistic talent, she said. She didn't say as much, but I wondered if she was also teaching her a few things in bed. I hoped they would become good friends, since Daisy needed that more than anything else. I longed for Daisy, to hold her in my arms again, and I remembered the last night we had spent together at home, our minds and bodies meeting and communicating in our own unique way. I wrote her a long letter that night.

Although my father had never approved of President Roosevelt, he didn't have much good to say about President Truman, either; I guess he was just a born Republican. He wrote sketchily but in his few words I felt his love for me and his general happiness with Martha, and that was enough. He reported that dignitaries were meeting in San Francisco to try to establish a United Nations, and he was very supportive of that.

For the first time I even began to think tentatively about home again, remembering the cool, dewy mornings when beginning work in the vineyards, the purpling of the green clusters on the thriving vines, the laborious harvest culminating in the first wine of the season, the restful tranquility of the valley in the noonday heat. I described it to Gerard, which led to his reminiscences of similar scenes in the apple orchards of Normandy before the war. Was the hell really to end? It was rumored that a peace with the Germans had already been signed by Eisenhower's Chief of Staff, but there had been no official announcement. After the years of war, the possibility of returning to that pastoral peace seemed almost unbelievable.

On May 8, early in the morning, we heard the jeep brake abruptly in front of the apartment and Blake began pounding on the door. Excitingly he burst in to report that we were officially at peace with Germany, that they had surrendered unconditionally in Berlin, and it was a day of celebration – they were calling it V–E Day.

"There will be a big parade downtown. Let's close the Clinic for the morning and join in!" he urged.

"Sure! – Gerard, how about coming along?" I hurriedly donned my best remaining uniform. "All of Amsterdam will be there – a day to remember always!" It would be his first day out of the apartment.

He shook his head. "I don't think I'm really ready for that – and all those people," he decided. "I'll wait here and have something ready for you both to eat, and maybe I can find a bottle of wine somewhere to add to the usual sausage."

Blake was anxious to go and returned to the jeep, no doubt remembering our entry into Paris the previous year. As usual I kissed Gerard on the doorstep, this time with more than my usual enthusiasm despite Blake's observation.

At first Gerard started to pull away. "I'm just a bag of bones," he murmured, but I pulled him close. "But you're *my* bag of bones," I grinned, pressing his lush lips to mine – not very original but the best I could do in a hurry.

I finally released him and started down the steps to the street. Out of the corner of my eye I caught a glimpse of a dark figure across the street, popping up from behind the ragged hedge, and the black barrel of a machine gun. A split second later my legs were slashed from under me by

193

a hail of bullets, and I crumpled to the sidewalk.

I was aware of a yell from Blake who jumped out of the jeep, pistol drawn, and I heard one shot before I lost consciousness. That's all it took to finish off my attacker, identified as Herr Oberstandartenführer Gunther, former commandant of the SS headquarters where our Clinic now operated.

He's in love with you, you know," Gerard said quietly.
"Blake? Oh, no, I don't think so. It's just that we've been through an awful lot together," I responded, trying not to grimace as Gerard rebandaged one of my wounds.

Blake was making house calls now. He had just left the apartment after checking the healing progress of my surgical wounds. After he had dispatched the SS sniper, he deposited me in the jeep and rushed me to the clinic where one of the doctors was just arriving. The clinic wasn't really set up for the kind of complicated surgery required to extract several bullets and patch up what was left of my legs, but they did an excellent job. That was a week ago.

Gerard smiled at me doubtfully. "You didn't see him snarl at the dead body of Oberstandartenführer Gunther or his tears when he picked up your mangled body to rush you to the clinic. Of course I followed the jeep to the clinic and observed him there, also."

"That must have been difficult for you, to enter that building again," I interrupted, thinking of the memories it must have revived.

Gerard pulled a fresh sheet over my bandaged legs, not looking directly at me. "Yes, but you were injured — I mean, now that it is a medical clinic, it is different — " I think he started to say that he had managed because he was concerned about me, but we had never spoken so directly before.

"And the way he shouted orders to the other medics, getting set up to operate on you — I could tell that they

195

were startled by his manner."

"He's getting his third stripe any day now, and I'm happy about that. I guess he was just acting like a Sergeant!"

"I also saw him kiss your forehead while you were unconscious and when nobody else was looking." That did surprise me.

"He always said he could be interested only in women."

Gerard smiled. "I can remember the time when I thought that way, also. We all must grow up sometime." He shrugged in the European way. "Women, men, we are all human and sexual − why should one be excluded?"

"Does it upset you that Blake and I are − close?"

Gerard looked at me for a long minute and then responded quietly, "I suppose I should be surprised if you weren't − close − after all you've been through together."

My heart warmed to the point that I had to break one of our unspoken rules. "You know I love you, don't you?"

He froze for a minute and did not respond immediately. Then he sat down in a chair next to the bed. He rested his head on my chest, his face turned away, and I forgot all about the pain in my legs. "Yes, and I love you." There, we had said it; it was no longer merely an assumption.

"But − " he continued, turning his somber face to me again, "the future is something else."

As usual I took the positive approach. "Doctor Morrison says I should regain full use of my legs," I began, "even though there may be some numb areas and they won't be very pretty − "

"I don't mean that. It really wouldn't make any difference − I mean, the war is over, except for the Pacific part, and you will soon be returning to the States − California, eight thousand miles away, isn't it?"

I hadn't really begun to think about that, but he was

right, of course.

"Will I ever see you again, after you leave?"

"Of course! There must be a way — " I would have to give it more thought. It was just like me to assume that everything would turn out well, even though that might not be realistic. It was inconceivable now that we would ever be separated.

It was time to change the subject. "Do you understand why Gunther shot me? Was he really aiming for you?"

Gerard rose and started clearing away the discarded bandages. "No, I don't think so. The neighbors said they were suspicious that he had been hiding in one of the abandoned houses across the street for several days. I think he tracked me here and saw you and me together, kissing — I am not sure."

"Do you think he was jealous of us? Really?"

He nodded slowly. "Gunther had a lot of hate in him, but I think he actually loved me, in his strange way. In thinking back over the weeks and months — in that basement room — I think it is possible that he could only show love in some seemingly distorted way." His memories were obviously difficult to endure, but he pressed on. "When I refused to show any affection for him, he tried to force me — and of course he was still unsuccessful — "

Over the next couple of weeks, while he nursed me through my recovery, he gradually divulged more details of his treatment at the hands of his SS captors, especially Gunther. The absolute horror of it came through as each detail was revealed. At first the questioning had been related to his suspected underground activities, but Gunther's interest gradually shifted to sexual gratification, and Gerard had been just as adamant in his resistance. This made Gunther furious, and he repeatedly raped his mouth and his ass, interspersed with whippings and beatings.

197

A few times he had brought other prisoners to the cell, torturing them while Gerard was forced to watch, actually hoping that these atrocities would increase Gerard's respect for him and his authority. When the orders came for the SS to leave, to flee to escape capture from the Americans, they left him strapped to the table, expecting him to die of starvation.

Several times during those recitals my thoughts reverted to the discussions with Gerhard and Lili in Paris and the sensual titillation they expressed regarding sadistic–masochistic "play." Their romantic ideas about torture did not fit the reality of Gerard's experience. I also recalled my own perceptions, and the fantasies of giving and receiving pain that I had never fulfilled.

"Did any of this ever become erotically satisfying?" I asked. It required a little discussion before Gerard really understood what I meant, but then, after hesitating for a moment, answered, "Yes, I think it did, sometimes."

"Because of the way Gunther attacked you?"

It was apparent that Gerard had not really thought through this aspect of his trials as a prisoner, and he had to relive some of those experiences to answer my questions. It wasn't easy for him; I regretted bringing up the subject, and yet it seemed important.

"Once I concluded that Gunther was actually acting out of love," he said slowly, "it was possible for me to interpret his actions as love-making, sometimes. And sometimes I almost looked forward to his visits, knowing that I would be stimulated, that something would happen to dispel the solitary darkness hour after hour of that cell. Even pain at the hand of a lover is better than no 'love' at all."

I didn't really understand his reasoning then, but he took me another step along the way. "You may think that torture has no erotic element, but why do you have an erection if

198

that is true?" He grasped my rigidity through the sheet; until then I did not realize that I had become aroused by his accounting.

"Perhaps we can explore that situation sometime?" I ventured.

His eyes bore into mine and I knew that the seeds for loving in that mode had already been sown.

He pulled back the sheet and proceeded to do what he did so well, bringing me repeatedly to the point of orgasm with his mouth, then using his soothing hand for a minute, only to return to raise my fever again. I realized that there was a touch of sado-masochism there, a "pseudo-pain" that I sought masochistically and that he enjoyed producing. I could not tolerate it for long, because my legs developed more discomfort when I involuntarily twisted, but when I finally blasted off it was a tremendous relief. I had not realized how frustrated I had become since the shooting. I could also understand more easily the discomfort some of the soldiers in my care in the aid stations had experienced before my TLC, as Dr. Mills had termed it.

Later, when I was more comfortable, I persuaded Gerhard to straddle my face on his knees so I could pay homage to his beautiful shaft and its luxurious sheath. I was reminded of the soldier who said he had dreamed of sex even while in the trenches. Was his feeling of being a helpless victim, susceptible to maiming and death at the hands of other men in battle, a source of masochistic yearning for sex with men? Men who would not kill him but bring the "little death" of orgasm?

Gerard kissed me, and I held him tightly. "I never want to leave you," I murmured.

"If it weren't for me, Gunther would probably never have shot you," he reminded me, his eyes fixed at a distant point. I had discerned this feeling of guilt before, but perhaps it would always remain to some extent. Then he turned to look at me again, his customary smile in place. "At least now I have the opportunity to care for you as you cared for me only a few weeks ago."

The next time Blake came to check on my progress he brought Dr. Morrison with him. They spent a long time, poking and prodding and grunting at each other, and finally Dr. Morrison pulled up a chair by the bed and looked grave.

"I'm afraid I've got some bad news. It seems there is infection in some of the wounds, and penicillin, even in large doses, is not effective. The long-term danger is developing a chronic bone infection, osteomyelitis. We can't handle that here. I think we ought to try to get you back to Walter Reed by hospital plane, the sooner the better."

My last few days in Amsterdam, waiting for the plane to the States, were difficult for all of us. My primary concern was Gerard.

He was unable to find his parents at or near their home, and no one, their neighbors and friends that could be located, seemed to know if they were still alive. By accident he met a grocer whom he had known as a boy, who asked him to work for him in trying to restart his business now that some food was becoming available for legal sale again. He could live with the family. They had lost two sons in the war. It seemed a reasonable stopgap measure; at least he would not be alone.

Blake tried, as a favor to me, to discover the mechanisms for bringing a Dutch citizen to the states. The only provision that seemed to have been set up was for newly married wives of American servicemen, for the most part English, who would be cleared for immigration, but of course there was no bureaucratic pigeon-hole for Gerard.

My wounds were beginning to smell from the infection − even I was aware of it − but Gerard slept with me my last night in the former officer's apartment. Of course we didn't sleep very much. Both of us refused to accept separation as an alternative. We tried to convince each other that it would work out, that we would manage to find a way to bring Gerard to the states soon, very soon − . I was wretched with loneliness for him at the same time my mouth was full of him.

When the truck arrived to transport me to the plane, the whole crew was there to see me off. Gerard and I had said our goodbyes in the apartment, but there was still the question of Blake. Our bond was strong, especially when going through the hell that Blake and I had faced together, and it was a wrench to think that we might not meet again. His eyes welled with tears as he shook my hand, and then he embraced me in a bear hug until I wondered about my ribs standing up under the strain. His muscular chest felt good in my arms. Sex wasn't the answer to everything.

"You'll soon be able to go home and finally make it up with that girl of yours, the one I've heard so much about," I gulped.

"Sure," Blake croaked, "and after we get married we'll come to see you in Napa, too, one of these days."

The medics pretended to be interested elsewhere, obviously embarrassed. Even Gerard recognized that we needed privacy at that moment. Blake still had something he wanted to say.

"Matt, I just want you to know — well — that morning, after we took that direct hit on the station in France — when I found you in the middle of all the debris, your arms around what was left of Dr. Mills, your face wet with tears — I made up my mind that I was going to try to take his place for you. I mean — oh, hell — I knew I couldn't really take his place but — make up for the loss as much as I could. . . . "

By this time we were both crying. "And you did, too, guy — I'll never forget — " What could I say to my best friend, my major link with sanity through that endless year of horror and death?

"I'll be sure to have a prime wine for you whenever you show up in Napa," I tried to grin to turn off my tears. I never was able to coax a smile from him, but at least his eyes brightened a little as if a cloud had lifted.

The truck driver was getting nervous to be underway; I was wheeled into the back of the hospital truck and that's when I began to experience for myself the helplessness and the frustration of being a patient unable to get around on his own — I had been on the other side of that situation for what seemed like forever. Perhaps the very impersonality of the event helped in my separation anxiety from Gerard — there was no choice; get over it. We would survive, somehow.

It took a couple of days, of course, before I was actually in a hospital bed at Walter Reed, and that was the beginning of my experience of being an "object of medical concern," as the nurse expressed it. Actually I fitted into a protocol that had been developed for people like me with persistent infections to try out some new antibiotics in the research pipeline. Medical treatment was combined with surgical debridement, and I was able to move around carefully, sometimes walking with assistance. Mild exercise probably helped, the doctors thought, to keep the wounds draining and encourage regrowth of bone to fill in the spaces.

The negative side of my infections was that I was confined to my room because they were afraid my bugs might contaminate other patients who were having enough trouble as it was. After living with other men constantly for several years and thinking sometimes that I would give anything to be by myself, adjustment to a private room was surprisingly difficult. At least it offered a chance to catch up on fiction reading which I had seriously missed. It was the only activity that could keep my mind from dwelling on Gerard and my longing for him.

I called home and talked to my father but did not encourage him to travel to Washington. He had never flown and I could tell he had trepidations about it. I expected to be discharged soon, and we agreed to postpone a reunion until it could be final.

About the first of August, the nurse came in the room

203

with an officer trailing behind. "You have a visitor, and he's from the Pentagon!"

I looked over her shoulder at the special insignia of the Medical Service Corps Captain behind her. All I knew about the MSC was that they were not doctors but with scientific or medical administration skills, but then I looked at his face and looked again. "Wes! For God's sake, I never thought I would see you again!"

The nurse looked very disapproving at my informal reception of the officer, but then Wes pushed past her and shook my hand delightedly. "Matt, it's good to see you!" He turned to the nurse. "You might invite a few more people in for a little ceremony we're going to have," he suggested.

"What?" I asked.

"Oh, just a little presentation," Wes smiled. I had always considered the lines in his face attractive and now they had deepened, I saw. There were a few gray hairs in his temples, but he was as trim and handsome as ever. He continued holding my hand, and it felt good – warm and strong.

When a few other patients and a couple of nurses had crowded into the room, he began the "ceremony," presenting me with some of the usual medals that everyone taking part in the European action would receive, but topped it off with a presentation of the Purple Heart. He read a whole paragraph of glowing description, but I didn't really take it all in. He pinned all the medals on my rather scruffy pajama shirt. I was speechless. Everyone applauded, congratulating me for whatever they thought I had done, and then left. Wes sat in the chair next to the bed.

"That was you who was involved with that mysterious professor, wasn't it?" I was finally able to ask.

Wes nodded, and I could see his mind flip back to

another time. "Professor von Osterhaus was, at one time, a noted physicist whom we tried to recruit for a project, along with many other European scientists. We could never be sure that he was agreeable to working with the allies or was actually loyal to a foreign government. At one time it was very important that we discover where he stood, because he had information that was vital to both sides."

"And you were working on that 'project,' even when we were stationed together here at Walter Reed?"

Wes nodded. "Even now we have not included any mention of your activity in that episode because — well, it is still confidential. At least for a few more days."

"Huh?"

He ignored my question. "So tell me about yourself — the nurse tells me that you are about ready to go home, back to 'Napa,' I suppose?"

I nodded. "So they say. The infections are much improved and I think they need this bed. There is only one draining site now, and that should clear up soon without any special care. I have just one real problem — "

"Yes?"

Would he think me juvenile to be pining for my lover in Amsterdam? There was reason to believe that Wes would understand. I knew that he had felt strongly about me at one time. Finally I told him all about Gerard and what our separation meant to us. As I outlined the story I realized it might sound like a strange romantic but unrealistic fairy tale, but I am sure he could tell from my face that it was vitally important to me, to us. His eyes never left mine until I had finished.

"Do you have any suggestions? You're at the Pentagon, you know your way around Washington, and I don't, of course," I concluded.

Wes gazed pensively out of the window at the shimmering sunshine and the green grass stretching across the campus. It was hot in the room but Wes was cool and concentrated. "There might be a chance — a window in time when it might work," he finally mused. "Give me all the details, his full name, his present address, and I'll see what we might arrange. It would be easy if only the State Department were involved. Working with the Immigration Service is always difficult, but maybe — " He gripped my hand as in the old days. It was the same hand that had fondled me in the hotel bed eons ago, in another world.

After he left I had difficulty taking up where I had left off in my book. All the pain and longing for Gerard had come flooding back in my recital to Wes, but at least there was some hope, now that Wes had promised to look into it.

My doctors set August 8 for my discharge day, and I was given an appointment for my "separation" from the Army the next day, but on August 6 my expectations were eclipsed by one of the most important events of the century. American planes dropped an atomic bomb on Hiroshima, and the world would never be the same again.

I had been taken off infection precautions that morning, so my room became a rallying point for other soldiers, recovering like me from their exposure to the disastrous war. Surely the Japanese would surrender now, and the war would finally be over! Everybody could go home — except those hundreds of thousands who would never go home again. Truman was everyone's hero for making the right decision to use the bomb despite the horrendous cost in Japanese lives. The end was in sight.

But the next morning's newspaper and radio broadcasts did not carry news of the Japanese surrender. General MacArthur was making confident noises, but apparently the Emperor had not yet decided to admit defeat. For the first time the term "Manhattan Project" was mentioned officially in connection with the atomic bomb.

I was sitting in my chair that afternoon when Wes appeared again and this time he had a visitor with him. The nurse followed him into the room, but he gently excluded her. "We need to do a little de-briefing," he explained — whatever that meant. He locked the door and turned to the other visitor, a sergeant whom I had assumed was his aide. "I don't think I have to introduce you two," he murmured.

The sergeant ducked out from behind Wes' form. "Matt, the sexiest surgical tech in the class! How the hell are you?"

"Claude Marcel!" My jaw almost struck the floor. It seemed he was always turning up at the most unexpected moments.

He gave a little dance step, as if he were being introduced on stage in full drag costume, flinging one arm in the air and ending by performing a curtsy. I think I detected a subtle hint of mascara around his always suggestive eyes.

"Behave, now," Wes muttered to him, placing his arm around his shoulder. Claude's arm went around Wes' waist as they beamed at me, waiting for my reaction. "I have to be careful where I go with him," Wes chuckled affectionately.

"Wait a minute," I said, my brain finally functioning. "You two? Lovers?" I slumped backward in my chair in disbelief.

They both nodded happily. "Of course we have to be very careful about it," Claude almost giggled. "I still have a bunk and locker at the headquarters downtown, but Wes gets to live off the base and so it works out."

"Claude's been involved with scheduling USO tours overseas and even performing in some of them. All an offshoot of his performance in Irving Berlin's play and movie." He gave Claude a little kiss on the forehead, and

207

my gut twisted. It took a moment to decide that my angst was not due to the obvious love between Wes and Claude, but because I missed Gerard so much. Their affection had stirred up my own emptiness.

"But let's get down to business," Wes proposed. He and Claude sat on the bed, side by side, while Wes, his face grave but his eyes sparkling like a conspirator in a spy movie, explained the "business."

"Even as we speak," he began stentorianly, sounding a little like a pontificating Orson Welles, "our agents are entering the grocery establishment of one Wolfje van Beek in Amsterdam, The Netherlands, in search of an individual we will call 'Gerard,' although that is not exactly the correct pronunciation." I hadn't told him about the problem in pronouncing his name so he must have learned that on his own. Still in his mock seriousness: "Said Gerard will be instructed to gather his meager belongings together and be ready to board a silver flying machine, otherwise known as a U.S. Military Air Transport Service plane, along with others of various persuasions, at a designated time and bound for a designated destination, which in this case is Washington, DC."

"What?" I couldn't believe my ears!

Wes waved his hand at me; I was interrupting his recitation. Claude giggled happily as he watched my face light up.

"Upon arrival in said destination, he may encounter some confusion because of some peculiarities regarding his name, since only initials will have been used previously. Since his name is not pronounceable in American vernacular, that was considered sufficient grounds for a slight, uh, departure from the usual requirements." He was confusing me, but he continued.

"To counter this said confusion, a certain Captain Wesley

North of the U.S. Army currently attached to the Pentagon will be standing by to assist the U.S. Immigration and Naturalization Service, not generally recognized for their, ahem, perspicacity, with the documentation on said arrival. After which the said Gerard will be legally and irrevocably considered a legal immigrant as a war bride."

I was so astonished by all this that I couldn't speak. Claude again giggled irrepressibly, and I finally joined in with Wes' chuckling. The merriment must have been heard in the hall, and I suppose the nurse thought that it was a strange de-briefing indeed.

"It's the least we could do for our latest Purple Heart awardee," Wes added.

Claude jumped up from the bed and landed in my lap, his arms around my neck, and I tried to avoid a grimace from the sudden but brief pain that shot up my leg. He kissed me soundly on the lips, and Wes moved to stand beside me, smiling down at me, his arm around my shoulder. My incredible pleasure must have been obvious on my face.

"Wes, how can I ever — do you really think it will work?" I finally stammered.

"Sure it will! Everything has been carefully arranged in strict Pentagon style! With all the clamor and hysteria following the bombing of Hiroshima and with another bombing planned — well, let's just say that, with all the excitement, no one is paying too much attention to details these days."

Even as I looked incredulously into Wes' eyes, I was aware that Claude had begun to nuzzle my chest and lap the chest hairs. He was unbuttoning my pajama top and working his way down. A moment later he had slid to the floor between my legs and opened my pajama pants, his tongue following the opening to a burgeoning reception to

209

his amorous advances. There was nothing feminine about his appetite.

"Claude, you rascal!" I moaned as he began to engulf me. "In front of your lover, too!" Wes grinned at me and at his lover who was opening his throat lovingly for me. Obviously monogamy was not one of the rules of their relationship.

"He hasn't changed a whit!" Wes chuckled.

"I haven't either," I responded, reaching for Wes' fly. I hadn't finished unbuttoning it when I felt a swelling behind the gabardine, and a moment later I extracted the cause. I clutched his buttocks to me, still trim and firm as I remembered, and tried to swallow him whole. His happy moans joined with Claude's and mine in a scenario that must have been rare in a Walter Reed hospital room. It was just what I needed to prepare myself for the arrival of my "bride."

T oday we are celebrating the one-year anniversary of my discharge from the U.S. Army. It is also the anniversary of the atomic bombing of Nagasaki, but no one celebrates that. It may have played a role in obtaining clearance for Gerard that day in Washington, however.

As I lounge in the shade after our picnic lunch I also think back to the day, almost five years ago, in this same Napa community park with its still-muddy pond, when I first caught sight of handsome, sexy Craig who altered my life in so many ways. He still enters my thoughts occasionally when I catch sight of my son, Paul, his dark eyes brightening in some unique thought understood only by a four-year old. Craig would have been as proud of him as I am. Everyone has forgotten that he is not my biological son and no one mentions the circumstances of his birth and orphan status. Someday I'll tell him the whole story, but not soon.

Gerard is stretched out in the sun, sleek and muscular in his bikini, a solid citizen of the Napa Valley and the most beloved man in my life. By his side and a little uncomfortable in any position, beloved Daisy snoozes fitfully, awakened periodically by the movements of the unborn baby she carries. Those three people make my life more complete than I ever imagined possible.

When I brought Gerard home with me, I could only hope for the best, for the "family" I hoped to form. Thinking that discussion might do more damage than good, I introduced Daisy and Gerard with no conditions, no special preparations. I watched them together, watched them discover in each other the qualities I had previously discovered, and

211

when we shared our love and our bodies three ways it was the charmed beginning of the new family. Daily, Gerard and I work happily together, side by side, toiling with the land and the fruit it produces; Daisy makes a home for us, cares for our child, and shares our bed at night. The love among us three is always there.

The father of Daisy's baby is either Gerard or me, unless it turns out to be a twin pregnancy, in which case we might both have started a new individual. It does not matter which one of us is the father because we three are a family, and Paul will soon have a playmate; that is the important factor. At this moment the little guy is playing with other boys and girls in the sand, but he sometimes amuses himself for hours in solitary pursuits as well. I hope he never loses his independent spirit.

We joke with each other that we are all cripples of a sort: Daisy was crippled, traumatized by the lecherous priest, but seems to have forgotten those events; Gerard's faint scars from his brutal torture are largely haunting memories, but there are still nightmares; and my strong legs still bear the scars from the German Captain's irrational jealousy. Paul's trauma is hidden at the present, but may appear sometime in the future. We can deal with that, as a family. We are hopeful that we can prevent such trauma to our new child, but perhaps that is not totally realistic.

Trauma is not always totally destructive. Grapes must be crushed to become wine, their spirit, their life reappearing as sweet–tart bouquet for the palate. The ancients felt that wine was life-affirming and in its use there remains a connection, a continuum to the present; we as a family are nurtured by a valley that makes the grapes that make the wines.

We know well the influence that the setting for growth of the grapes has upon its ultimate delicacy. The slant of the sun, the warmth of the breeze, the time of the frost on our slope of the hill combine to create a characteristic vintage. Another slope of the same valley produces different wines. They are not necessarily inferior or superior, only different.

Some people may never understand us, a committed *ménage à trois*. They may not understand that love is not limited to the standard formula of husband and wife, or even same-sex lovers. It is not necessary that they understand us; they may be native to another slope where the sun strikes at a different angle and the fruit ripens differently, and the wine is − wine from a different slope.